The Painted Lighthouse

The Chronicles of

Burnam Tau'roh

Book Two

Also by Walter G. Klimczak

Falling in the Garden
This Place Only
My Forgotten Life
Blackberry Way
The Oak Hotel

Praise for *Falling in the Garden*

"...a magical miracle... involving time travel and alternate dimensions. The story is tightly plotted, with the mystery building quickly and smoothly. (An) enjoyable journey. The best kind of science fiction: The science sows the seeds, but the story grows the garden."

The Painted Lighthouse

The Chronicles of

Burnam Tau'roh

Book Two

Walter G. Klimczak

Autumn Harbor Press

Atlanta, GA

The Painted Lighthouse

The Chronicles of Burnam Tau'roh

Book Two

Autumn Harbor Press

March 2009

ISBN 978-0-578-01619-1

For more information about Autumn Harbor books,
please visit our website @ www.autumnharbor.com

This one is for Mom.

"This bridge will only take you half-way there, to those mysterious lands you long to see... The last few steps you have to take alone."

Shel Silverstein

Darkness reigns at the foot of the lighthouse.

Japanese Proverb

Many directions
In a dark and frozen sea
Are forever yours

The Pandiment of Time

Contents

Pronunciation Guide

Cast of Characters

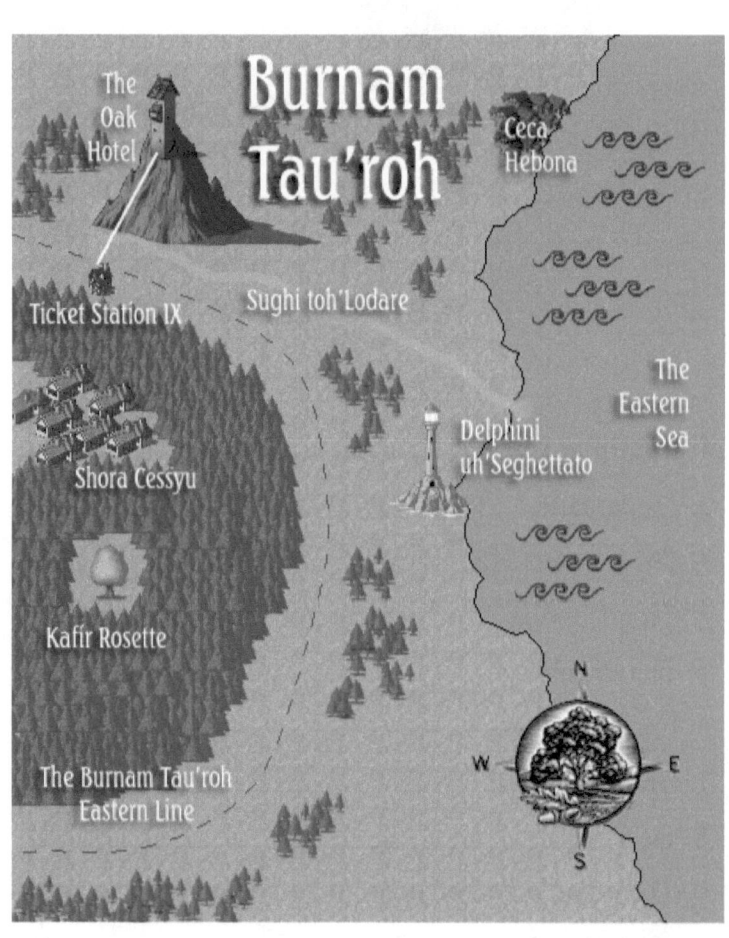

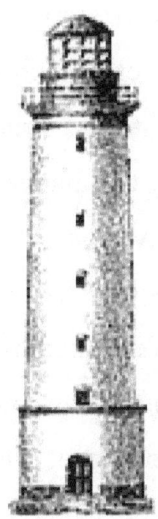

1. Return to Burnam Tau'roh

I t was definitely a stay-in-bed kind of morning—one best viewed from beneath a thick, goose-down quilt and through the drawn curtains of misted windows. For Lincoln Torres, there would be no snug bedcovers. The twelve year-old sat silent and motionless with his back against the base of the old hotel. Hugging bent knees to his chest, he stared anxiously out at the landscape before him. A sagging mantle of charcoal-grey clouds made the sky appear almost within reach. Rain was more than a simple promise; it was an unyielding guarantee.

The Oak Hotel, perched atop a cliff overlooking eastern Burnam Tau'roh, did not crouch from the miserable heavens above. A massive, multi-storied structure, this grand building was sentinel to everything that happened below. Its strength of presence was material as well, as it seemed to grow from the solid stone that marked its foundation.

The Sughi River (speaking in a muted, foamy roar from far below) rushed away from the base of the mountain toward the great Eastern Sea. Just south of the river's distant estuary, Lincoln could make out the white, vertical brushstroke of a lighthouse. Looking directly southward, a sprawling forest waited secretively behind Ticket Station IX. Lincoln recalled how he and Kayleigh had made their way through the woods to the creepy town of Shora Cessyu. The now silent tracks of the Burnam Tau'roh Eastern Rail Line ran like the dry remains of a snake-shed to the southeast. Listening, Lincoln did not hear the sound of BTEL #3, the train that had transported them down the line and had spoken to them as if alive.

And to think I came from this land! he mused. He recalled the old librarian explaining that, as a baby, he had been found alone in a boat on Autumn Harbor Bay. There was but one item with him in the small dinghy, other than the blanket covering his small body—a copy of *The History of Burnam Tau'roh.*

What now? he wondered. Having arrived hours ago in the young pine forest that covered the posterior side of this small mountain, Lincoln was painfully aware of his impossible circumstances. He knew there was a greater good to serve, but the only thing he saw before him was Kayleigh. He *needed* to find Kayleigh.

"Lincoln?" a soft, female voice called out.

Heart racing at the thought of being caught so early on, Lincoln scanned the mountaintop and focused on the figure emerging from the cylindrical conveyance known as SkyCarOne. Through the mist, a small, thin form moved steadily toward him. Stumbling to his feet, he couldn't believe his luck at finding Kayleigh so quickly. After a few steps toward her, however, he stopped. She wore a dark, grey robe with a hood pulled loosely over her head. Slowly, two pale hands reached up and pushed the hood back. Lincoln beheld a young woman in her early twenties. Her features were soft, but her bright, green eyes demanded his attention.

"You're not—" he began.

"No," she said, almost apologetically, "I'm not Kayleigh, but I know where she is and I want to help. Quickly, go back to where you were sitting and make yourself still."

Confused, Lincoln did as he was told. As he set his back against the hotel, the front door burst open and a voice filled with menace bellowed, "Sheenie! You have good news, I hope?"

"Yes, Truman. Everything at the Cinema is locked down. Creek is still secure on the lower level. He's not going anywhere."

"Excellent," hissed Truman Stitch. Lincoln could almost see his eyes, reflecting not only his own dark soul, but the cancerous glare of Ka Tolerates as well. He could feel the dark energy pulsing outward in heavy, leaden waves.

"Are you still planning to leave at sunset?" Sheenie asked. It was at this point when Lincoln realized that her name sounded familiar. It didn't take much searching to recall that she was the woman he and Kayleigh had heard outside the closet just before their first journey to Burnam Tah'roh.

"I'd leave now, but we still need the suspension draught."

Just the sound of Stitch's voice caused Lincoln to cringe.

"Will it be delivered to the hotel?" Sheenie asked.

"Yes. You might as well stay here and wait. Pay for it with this." Truman tossed a coin through the air and Sheenie caught it without hesitation.

"Our mission is nearly complete," he said with a thick smile. "We will finally be... free to explore other possibilities."

"Yes, Truman," she replied, standing her ground, showing no fear or trepidation.

The front door swung shut with dark finality. Sheenie stood where she was for the count of ten, then allowed her braced shoulders to relax. She walked toward Lincoln, helped him up with one outstretched hand and led him around the building to an area beneath the back stairway. Lincoln could not get over her green eyes. They held power and control, though understanding as well.

"I'm unsure where to begin," she said as, together, they backed secretively into the shadows.

Shaking his head slightly, Lincoln asked, "Is Kayleigh okay?"

"Yes. Kayleigh is inside the hotel as we speak. She's safe... for the moment. Truman is preparing to take her back to our world. Delivering her might cancel out the fact that he and I were not able to bring back the Pilgrims, as was our primary mission."

"Emil told us about some of that. I found out more from the glass spheres on Te'hæra Thorn."

The young woman's eyes sparkled. "I so wish that I could have been there. You were actually in Kana Hove?"

"I was there a couple of days before I figured out how to leave."

"Truman wasn't very talkative when he returned. I noticed the change instantly. That's why I'm speaking to you now instead of turning you over to him. I'll admit that he and I have taken advantage of our situation here in Burnam Tau'roh. I'm not proud of it, but I'll admit my own faults. When he returned, though, I knew that he had done the unspeakable. I could read it in his eyes. He had touched the last tree of the valley. I still can't believe it, Lincoln. I've followed him every step of our timeless journey, but here is where I get off. Once he returns to Atoth with Kayleigh, he plans to beg for mercy. Whether or not this is given, he intends to use his new power to take control of our governing system and use it as a stepping stone to greater gain. He has made many connections here in this backwater province, but this has only been a testing ground."

"I don't understand," Lincoln said.

"Truman has been running illegal trade between parallel worlds. For those willing to pay, he can hunt down items not found in one world and pull them over into another. Burnam Tau'roh is the crossroads for this trade. Autumn Harbor is the main port of transfer into your world. He has found quite a few wealthy people on your side interested in such things.

"Truman, however, has no lust for money. It is all about power. He has broken many laws and traded for certain high technologies that have not and will not be invented in this world or yours."

"Like the computer panel in the book that lets us travel between worlds?" Lincoln asked.

"Well… yes. That book, however, has caused many problems. We still don't know where it came from or how the transposition panel came to be part of it. Truman has hunted down many copies of this book and tampered with the panel, but it's still anomalous."

"Did Truman do something to the panels so Emil couldn't travel through them?"

Frowning, Sheenie spoke quickly, "You know far more than I imagined, but we can't continue talking like this. Truman needs to be certain I'm still on his side. Wait here for one hour, then go up these stairs and find Mona Tarok. She is quite upset at having us here at the Hotel and seeing you will lift her spirits. Truman will be gone by then and won't return until it's time for him to leave."

"You're not going with him?"

"I believe that he is done with me, Lincoln Torres. He wants me to remain here and keep my eyes open, but I don't think he intends to return. He is moving on to other, more horrible things. I will remain his spy no longer. There are things he has done here in Burnam Tau'roh that I wish to repair. There are people he has taken advantage of that I wish to make amends with."

She stood and took a deep breath.

"Kayleigh is in the basement of the hotel in a room filled with Trokamano crates."

"Troka—what?"

A loud thud caused them both to jump, then Truman's voice called out for Sheenie.

"Mona will help you as much as she can. Good luck!"

With that, Sheenie took off around the side of the hotel. Lincoln sat silently, wondering how exactly he was going to count off an hour's time with any accuracy. He reached into his pockets and pulled out three items from his first visit in Burnam Tau'roh. The first was the brass coin. One side held the image of a large tree and the other a lighthouse. The second was the tiny bottle. It was no larger than his thumb, the glass thick and darkly tinted; a slim cork was tied to the neck. The final item was the note Mona had given them from the strange guest who had taken ill. He held these things and thought of Kayleigh. It was maddening that he had to wait down here with Kayleigh so close by. It was by sheer force of will that he remained sitting. A persistent urge to stand and move filled his veins. *Go*, a voice inside told him. *Go now and get her before something happens and it's too late!*

Waiting, waiting... but for how long, really?

"I'm sorry, Kayleigh," he whispered to his knees. "I'm right outside and I want to come in but I can't. I have no idea how much time has gone by. Ten minutes? Thirty? Has it already been an hour?"

Lincoln stretched and yawned, then smacked his forehead with an opened palm. Why didn't he just count the seconds and minutes off in his mind? But what good would counting do now?

Still, because there was nothing more to be done, he began to whisper, "One, two, three..."

A fragrant wind blew against the hotel, carrying the scent of the pines that grew along the mountainside, sweetened by the sea that swelled not-so-far away.

Lincoln counted.

And then, without meaning to, he fell asleep.

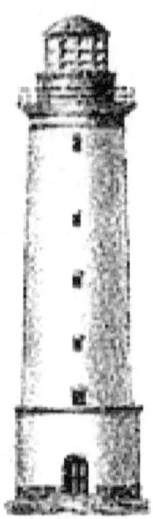

2. Trokamano

incoln felt as if he had been floating in some dark, thick liquid when two arms pulled him quickly up and out of it. It didn't take long to comprehend that the liquid had been *sleep* and the rescuer *Mona Tarok*.

"You must follow me," she whispered impatiently. "Quickly."

With what felt like a lump forming in his heart, Lincoln realized the sun had traveled almost the entire arc of the sky. He had slept through the remainder of the morning and most of the afternoon!

Scampering up the zig-zag stairway that clung against the backside of the hotel, Lincoln followed the familiar women upward, doing his best not to lean in the wrong direction. With sleep still clinging to his hazy mind, he feared slipping and falling back down to the hard ground. When they reached the door at the top, Lincoln allowed the hotel to swallow him. Immediately, he felt at peace. This was not, he realized, his most informed emotion since Stitch could be anywhere. Still, he allowed the rich aroma of the wooden walls, ceiling and floor to set his body at ease. Spaced at even intervals on the walls were small, powder-blue ovals that gave off just enough light to see by. Lincoln realized that he remembered this blue light from his last visit, but hadn't inquired about it.

They stopped before a closed door in some darker, unlit hallway.

"All those blue lights…" he began "What powers things in this place?"

Mona reached out and ran her fingers across a run of numbers that had long ago been engraved into the door. She smiled and turned to the boy, whispering:

"Mayor Stitch brought the blue lights and *ForeverBatteries* to Burnam Tau'roh many years ago. Strange people came and told us it wasn't safe to use this power and threatened to take the Mayor away. They were very short people and dressed oddly. I'm not sure what happened to cause them to leave, but the Mayor told us all we must use the batteries discreetly. He collected most of the blue ovals that were sold and charged me with filling the hotel with them. They turn on only when they are needed."

Mona Tarok pushed in at the door, revealing a long, rectangular room within. Quite different from other rooms he'd seen before in the Oak Hotel, Lincoln saw it must be some sort of laundry room. Sliding bins (all open) lined one wall. Darkness filled the chutes behind them.

"Is this where you bring the dirty clothes?" he asked.

"Years ago, when there was never a vacancy here at the Oak Hotel, this was the most active room... besides my kitchen, of course. Bed linens and clothing were sorted and sent down to be cleaned in vats of hot water in the basement."

She paused, then spoke in a more conversational tone:

"It is good to see you again, Lincoln. I was so worried about you and Kayleigh when you left that morning. I tried to keep Truman from following you, but could put him off for only so long. So much has changed since then."

"I think he would have found us no matter what," Lincoln said, recalling with a shudder the way Stitch had simply raised his hand and made Kayleigh disappear.

Mona moved quickly to a shelf in the corner and returned with a light, woolen overcoat. She held it out to Lincoln.

"Put this on," she said. When Lincoln shrugged the oversized garment on, he laughed at the length. The bottom reached past his knees.

"I'm a little confused," he said, then noticed the older woman eyeing one of the nearby laundry chutes.

"No way," Lincoln said, his smile fading. "You want me to go down one of those things? We're like, near the top of the hotel. Didn't you say these tubes went down to the basement?"

"I want nothing more than to sit here and speak with you, Lincoln. If I had my way, you, Kayleigh and I would be sitting in the kitchen discussing all that has happened over an early dinner. Unfortunately, Kayleigh is about to be taken very far from here. If Stitch succeeds, there is little chance we'll ever see her again. By entering the basement this way, there is little chance that Stitch will see you."

"Okay, I get your point. But won't Stitch be expecting something like this? He outguessed us every step of the way the last time we were here."

Frowning, Mona's voice darkened, "I don't think we'd be able to pull off something like this with the old Stitch around. The creature that returned, however, is both more powerful, yet less... *aware* of the more mundane things around him. It seems to be the only thing we can play to our advantage. I've spoken with Sheenie. I never had reason to trust the woman, but—as I've said—things have changed. Between the two of us, Stitch will believe that he has Kayleigh secured with him for the trip home. Now..."

Buttoning up the long, soft jacket, Lincoln moved toward one of the open bins. Mona joined him near the dark aperture.

"Take this," she said, handing him a dull, brass key. "Until now, only I have known about the secret landing near the river. You should be able to slip away easily. The door is small and low to the ground, in the same room you'll find Kayleigh in."

Without asking for further clarification, Lincoln pocketed the key, gave Mona a quick hug, then hauled himself up above the opening (holding on to a narrow, wooden eave above it) and entered feet first.

The trip down was much quicker (yet lasted longer) than he expected. In retrospect, Lincoln decided it might have been smarter to go head-first and carefully crawl his way to the bottom. As his body jetted downward, the fear of getting stuck, his body wedged into a blocked or broken area, caused his heart to thud erratically.

His landing was accomplished as such: the tunnel leveled off without warning and the chute sent his body careening off the edge of a large wooden table. Lincoln managed to stop himself from tumbling over by leaning back and spreading his arms out just as his bottom and legs smacked the floor. He probably slid a good ten feet before stopping.

Standing slowly, cautiously, Lincoln was amazed he hadn't crashed into one of the dozens of wooden crates that filled the room. Taking a deep breath (now that his breathing had returned to normal), he smiled at the familiar, yet exotic aroma of citrus. He moved to the nearest crate and read the two words stenciled onto its side: TROKAMANO ORCHARDS. These same words appeared on each of the crates.

And then he remembered the person he had come down here for.

"Kayleigh?" he whispered.

No answer.

"Kayleigh?" he asked a bit louder this time.

This time, a muffled reply came from somewhere in the center of the room:

"Here," a voice spoke, though it sounded far-away.

"Make a noise that I can follow," Lincoln requested.

Immediately, a metered tapping began. He followed it to a crate labeled TROKAMANO RAPTURE FIGS, leaned down and spoke into the dark area between the wooden slats:

"Kayleigh? Are you okay?"

"As soon as you get me out of here, I'll be fine," was her reply.

A quick search revealed nothing that might help him tear the boards from the box.

"How did Truman seal the crate?" Lincoln asked.

"It wasn't with nails or anything like that. He just put the top on, but I haven't been able to push it back open.

Studying the lid, Lincoln soon discovered several notches that had been pushed into the walls of the crate. Thumbing each of them back was easy work and he carefully raised the lid. Kayleigh stood hesitantly, eyes darting around the room. She allowed Lincoln to lift her out.

Standing before her, Lincoln felt his chest tighten. He reached out and pulled her close. They held each other tightly, not saying anything for a moment. Finally, Kayleigh whispered, "I thought you'd be stranded on Te'hæra Thorn forever."

"What Stitch did to you…"

"He didn't hurt me," she said. They were looking into each other's eyes with their foreheads nearly touching. "He just… moved me. When I opened my eyes, I was resting on a cot at The Oak Hotel. I remember seeing Mona and Sheenie, but I was very sleepy. I don't know how I got there, but I woke up in that crate."

A thunderous boom shook the hotel and they dropped to their knees.

Pulling the brass key from his pocket, Lincoln held it up to show her.

"Mona gave this to me. Something about a door near the floor."

Though the loud sound did not repeat itself, they remained low, crouching. Lincoln led the way across the room to the nearest wall. Searching with fingers as well as eyes, Lincoln began to question the veracity of this *secret* door. It was Kayleigh who spotted it first. The grain of wood between the door and wall met perfectly—it was easy to see how it could have been overlooked.

Unlocking the door, they passed into the hidden channel and in less than a minute arrived at another door that pushed open onto a small outdoor landing. The river ran alongside it, softly at this point, yet they could hear the louder rush of water in the distance.

"Man," Kayleigh breathed, "If we're at the river, then that room with the crates isn't on the first floor of the hotel like I thought."

"More like a few hundred feet straight down," Lincoln added.

Turning, they saw that the door they exited was, indeed, affixed to a wall of stone. Looking up, they watched the sheer rise of the cliff wall extinguish itself thirty feet above in mist. The water before them moved from left to right. The only other object on the wedge of land they stood upon was a small boat.

"Mona said we'd be able to *slip away easily*," Lincoln intoned. He moved toward the aft end of the boat and began to untie a rope from a steel ring embedded in the stone wall. Free from the cliff, they managed to push the small craft near the edge of the water. Kayleigh climbed in first, then Lincoln. Using oars they found wedged in the bottom of the boat, they pushed away from the shore.

With barely a sound, they shot forward, speeding into the evening dusk, bobbing slightly to and fro and putting wonderful, glorious distance between them and Stitch.

3. The Painted Lighthouse

The shoreline at port and starboard drifted by in muted shades of green and grey. The sound of the river and the chuckling it made against the hull of the boat were both welcomed.

"I never thought I'd see you again," Lincoln whispered.

"I knew you'd come," Kayleigh replied at once, and Lincoln could almost see her smile. He reached out and helped to pull her toward the center of the boat. She sat beside him and allowed herself the indulgence of leaning against him while wrapping her arms gently around his shoulders. "You would never let him take me away."

"I did on Te'hæra Thorn."

"There was nothing you could have done then. But you came back for me. That's the important thing."

Lincoln didn't know what else to say. The simple act of sitting there, feeling her beside him, was something beyond words. For the span of endless minutes, they breathed deeply of the fresh, moist river air. Finally, Kayleigh couldn't help but ask, "Okay, so what's the plan. Seeing as you're actually getting away with breaking me out, what's next?"

Lincoln quickly explained what had happened to him after she was abducted by Stitch. He told her about his quiet days in Kana Hove, how he escaped from the quiet planet through the remains of Ka Tolerates and returned to Autumn Harbor. Kayleigh accepted everything until he told her about Lea Ruttier, the town librarian.

"She actually knew my Grandfather?" she asked dubiously.

"He kind of put her in charge when he left Autumn Harbor. She's been watching over us. She told me that your Grandfather thought we'd be the ones to bring back the de'Malange. The last thing she said was that we needed to find a boy named David Grey on the coast of the Eastern Sea."

"That's kind of vague," Kayleigh said.

"That's what I said. Unfortunately, the police came and there wasn't any more time to talk. She told me where to find another copy of *The History*, which was how I got back here. Oh, she also said that I might have been born here in Burnam Tau'roh. I was only found in Autumn Harbor when I was a baby."

Kayleigh was silent for a while. Lincoln was about to speak when she said, "So it's not just me then. With a connection, I mean."

"I guess not. But we still haven't found your grandmother."

"My grandfather said she might be here in Burnam Tau'roh."

"We'll just have to keep our eyes open, then."

Neither knew when their words began to slide into nonsense. The border between the wakeful world and dreams was not well defined. Their sleep, however well deserved, was short-lived. The boat slid noisily up onto a sand bar not far from the estuary that would have dumped them out into the softly rolling Eastern Sea. It wasn't the sound of the boat on the pebbly shore that caused them to start awake, but rather the raucous peal of laughter and merriment. Lincoln stood up first, helping Kayleigh to her feet. Pulling the boat further up onto the narrow beach, they then pushed it into a dense stand of sea oats in an attempt to conceal it. Light spilled out over the dunes before them along with a rising din of voices.

"It's got to be close to midnight, no?" Lincoln asked.

Kayleigh held a finger to her lips as they moved toward the crest of the dune. Rising into the night beyond it was the lighthouse, reflecting the glow of hidden, colored lights. At once, they were engulfed by a roiling sea of partygoers. The mass of people were dressed in a bizarre assortment of colors and styles. Lincoln could now hear music, though from where it came he could not tell. A striking woman, wearing a dress with ever-changing cascades of color, moved close to him and took him suddenly by the hands; they performed two slow turns before she let go and melted into the crowd. Slightly dizzy and surprised, Lincoln had to search for Kayleigh. He found her standing only a few feet away, smiling.

"I didn't know you could dance!" she shouted above the noise, laughing.

Together, they moved toward the lighthouse. It took longer than it should have as they pushed inconstantly through the chaos around them. Reaching the whitewashed outer wall, Kayleigh held out her palm and pressed it against the lighthouse.

"It almost doesn't seem real," she said, looking up.

Lincoln knew what she meant, though not exactly why. It felt as if they were dreaming. The entire scene felt fluid and unreal. Lincoln imagined the lighthouse was something alive and only appeared to be created from stone.

Just as they reached the steps that led to the front entry of the structure, a man jumped in front of them, holding a long, black cane. His face had been painted in long, vertical stripes of black, white and pink. His lips were pure black and his teeth milk white. Spinning the cane in a fast, clockwise rotation, he bowed slightly before speaking:

"You are friends of Madame Chamberlain, I presume?"

It was Kayleigh who found the nerve to answer, "We do not know Madame Chamberlain, but we are friends, kind Sir."

The man laughed aloud, put an arm around Kayleigh and led her toward the front steps. Lincoln followed and they all sat, grounding themselves as the revelers moved as a great, surging wave around the lighthouse.

"I'm Kayleigh and this is Lincoln," Kayleigh said.

The music, they now realized, came through the open lighthouse door as well as its many windows.

"My name," the man began, his smile deepening, "is Sagan Rideau. I must tell you up front that I have been charged with the unhappy job of turning away trespassers and gatecrashers.

This is, after all, the biggest private celebration we have this time of year."

"We're not crashing your party," Lincoln said, "We're actually just—"

"Lincoln?" Kayleigh interrupted.

Sagan Rideau looked back and forth between them, a knowing smile on his lips.

"Do not worry, children," he whispered confidentially. "I will not turn you in. If it is within my power, might I not be able to help in some way?"

Kayleigh and Lincoln considered this. Again, the question: to trust or not to trust? Hadn't Stitch fooled them countless times pretending to be people he was not?

It was Lincoln who tested with a simple statement. "We're looking for someone named David Grey."

Kayleigh tensed. The name David Grey was, truly, the only lead they had. Still... in order to advance they needed to confide in someone.

They sat silently, awaiting an answer. The striped man appeared to taste Lincoln's words as if they were a rich dessert, not ready to comment until he'd had another bite. The music from the lighthouse changed to a slower, more solemn waltz. The throng of people slowed.

Kayleigh bit down slightly on her lower lip, then looked at Lincoln. "Do you still have those things that we got from Mona?"

Smiling, Lincoln reached into his pocket. Pushing aside the miniature glass bottle and note, he reached down further and pulled out the coin.

"We were given this," Lincoln began, handing the well-worn coin to Sagan. "We're not sure what it means, but it might mean something to you considering where we are."

The older man took the coin and his eyes widened instantly. On one side of the coin was the soft engraving of an oak tree. The flip side showed a lighthouse that may have been identical to the one now towering above them.

"Where did you get this?" he whispered.

"It was left behind at The Oak Hotel," Kayleigh said. "The Cook there thought it might have been meant for us."

Sitting a bit straighter, Sagan's shoulders took a more confident posture.

"Well," he began, "If Mona Tarok passed this on to you, I'm sure it was with good reason. Though I believe, young lady, you should probably use a more respectful title than *cook* when referring to Madame Tarok."

"She's a good friend of ours," Lincoln put in, "We didn't know that you knew her."

Sagan laughed, "Know her? Who in Burnam Tau'roh doesn't? She's the only person in this province that has any sway with Mayor Stitch."

Noticing their expression at the mention of Stitch's name, Sagan whistled slowly through dry lips. "You're on the run from Truman Stitch, aren't you? No, don't get up. I said before that I won't turn you in and I'll stand by that. Here... come inside. This lot will be too drunk to dance within the hour, but they're safe. They'll be fine."

Oddly, the moment they passed over the threshold, the music grew much quieter. It was as if, Lincoln mused, the music came from the outer walls of the lighthouse itself. How this was accomplished, he could only guess.

Lincoln and Kayleigh noticed at once the murals painted upon the curving interior wall. It was hard to stop and focus on any one area—the intricate stories bled into one another with no seeming pattern. "It's as if," Lincoln said without thinking, his mouth open in abject wonder, "Someone opened up a book of fairy tales and let them loose."

Sagan grunted, then looked at Kayleigh. She, too, was staring at the murals in amazement. "You're kidding me?" he said, "You've never heard of Delphini uh'Seghettato? The great Painted Lighthouse? Why, it's in every baby's picture book..."

"Not in any book we would have seen," Kayleigh whispered absently, "We grew up... well, in a different place than this."

"You'd be surprised," Sagan chuckled darkly. "Things like this lighthouse, here... it doesn't matter what world you come from. If you looked closely enough, I'm sure you'd find hints of the lighthouse. Might just be a picture of it on the horizon, or a reflection in a mirror, but its there somewhere."

"Wait a minute," Lincoln said, turning toward him. "What do you mean which world we come from?"

"Young man, I've dealt with Traders from countless worlds here. Most of them go through Stitch, but a few come to see me. They use the floating bubbles of... well, I don't know what they're made of, but somehow they allow passage from this world into others. Some people float on through and don't know where they're going. Others have gadgets or special maps that tell them which bubble to go through next. You never know who will be coming through next."

Sagan explained that as far back as he could tell (before even Darian Gause, the keeper before him) there had been Traders, men and women from other worlds that appeared on the coast of the Eastern Sea. They would bring items that did not exist in this world. Items they would trade for things impossible to get in their own worlds. Truman Stitch, who had been Mayor of Burnam Tau'roh for countless years (and was considered by most either evil or an agent of evil) was the sole arbiter of these trades. Sagan admitted that with so many people advancing on the shores, a few interesting trades had come his way that Stitch knew nothing about. This happened often up and down the coast, as several small towns dotted the long shoreline.

"No guessing what Mayor Stitch would do if he happened upon any *outsider* trading," Sagan put in.

Turning to Lincoln, Kayleigh said, "I'll bet he spent all these years with Traders just looking for clues. Anything that would lead him to Emil."

"And those *History* books!" Lincoln said sharply, "Ms. Ruttier said she and Emil spent years trying to figure them out. Stitch had the one we left behind. Probably others, too, since he was able to get to Autumn Harbor."

"Autumn Harbor?" Sagan asked in a hushed tone.

"It's where we're from," Lincoln said.

"What does it mean to you?" Kayleigh asked.

"It's where Stitch does most of his trading. You see, when a ship pulls up to these docks loaded with merchandise, I'm to locate the Mayor immediately. He's usually here within the hour. He keeps a stash of things here at the lighthouse in case he finds something that interests him. Otherwise, the Traders go on their way either up or down the coast. Most stop here, though, so Truman can get first pick."

"Who does he trade with in Autumn Harbor?" Lincoln asked.

Just then, thunder boomed from somewhere outside. The three of them, recovering from the pure shock of the deafening sound, ran across the room to the door. Standing on the front steps, they found the assemblage of partygoers rising from the ground. All were looking up into the sky, their eyes wide and mouths agape.

Kayleigh and Lincoln followed their singular gaze and watched a hot, white trail trace slowly against the blue-black sky. It was moving quickly, rising in a west to east path. The sound it made was nothing any of them had heard before. The closest Kayleigh could imagine was icy water moving quickly through a long, glass tube. Lincoln felt his balance momentarily tilt and he almost fell down the lighthouse stairs.

"What could it be?" Sagan said, mirroring the very thought going through everyone's mind.

Kayleigh recalled the image of the horseshoe-shaped ship Emil had shown them with the vision beads. Squinting into the darkness, she thought she could make out a similar U shape. Lincoln remembered as well. He smiled. Mona and Sheenie had done it. Somehow, in some way, they had fooled Stitch into believing that Kayleigh was on board that ship. Without meaning to, he said aloud, "It's Truman Stitch. He's leaving this place forever."

And the crowd heard his words. At once, a massive cheer went up in the night. Why a group of strangers should listen to, let alone believe, the words of a stranger was beyond him. Still, the party seemed to take on an even more excited rhythm. There was simply an undeniable, inherent truth to his words.

By the end of the following day, nearly everyone in Burnam Tau'roh would hear the good news (which would officially be confirmed by Mona Tarok at The Oak Hotel) that Mayor Truman Stitch had left them for good.

It was a day not to be forgotten.

4. Ceca Hebona

incoln and Kayleigh left Sagan Rideau and the party at the lighthouse while it was still dark. Sagan had told them that it was possible someone named David Grey lived in a seaside town just a few miles to the north. He insisted they spend the night at the lighthouse and rest before setting out in the morning. Kayleigh almost relented, but

Lincoln felt uneasy being near the lighthouse. Also, as tired as he was, he still felt like they needed to be on the move.

"But Stitch is gone," Kayleigh pressed. "Don't we deserve a rest?"

Of course they did, but Lincoln stood his ground. An hour later, they began a sleepy, difficult walk up the dark coastline. The sound of the waves hushed away what sharpness of thought remained. The soft, airborne spray of the sea enrobed them in a soft mantle of dreams. They passed tufts of sea oats and other varieties of flora (which would certainly make fine temporary beds), but continued onward. Time meant nothing.

At some point in the lost center of night, they reached Ceca Hebona. The small, seaside town was anything but small. Every house and building had been raised above the beach by incalculable boards and rafters. An intricate system of boardwalks connected each structure and a massive marina and pier reached over the sea at its eastern side.

There was the soft, lonesome sound of bells tolling in buoys not far from the shoreline. The steady, dim strobe from the lighthouse miles down the beach was a devious paintbrush. They moved closer to what appeared to be an entrance—a steep, slanting ramp that led up onto the boardwalk. Along the edge of Ceca Hebona, down on the beach, were perhaps twenty boats all resting upside down on the sand.

Kayleigh followed Lincoln to one of these boats.

"We should be okay under here at least until morning," he said.

Kayleigh was in no mood to argue. Climbing up under the boat, they discovered several life preservers fashioned from rope and cork. Using these as pillows, they curled up closely in the darkness and at once fell asleep.

When they awoke, it was to the gentle sound of the sea. They remained undiscovered beneath the inverted boat. The sun, hot and white, burned like fire against the sand just outside their dark haven.

"Part of me wants to stay under here," Kayleigh said quietly.

And they did stay put, not saying much, for another five minutes.

"What if someone sees us coming out of here?" Kayleigh asked.

"We tell them we're boat inspectors sent by Mayor Stitch," Lincoln said, smiling.

Kneeling down, moving from cool to hot sand, they pushed under the boat and rolled out onto the beach. A large sign they had missed earlier announced:

CECA HEBONA:
THE FIRST BURNAM TAU'ROH
MARITIME SETTLEMENT

"I guess we're in the right place," Kayleigh said, shielding her eyes from the glare with cupped hands.

It was then that they heard something amazing. Something they hadn't heard in quite some time. Laughter—the free and joyful laughter of children. The sound brought immediate smiles to both Kayleigh and Lincoln. And, as if this sound were a personal greeting and welcome from the seaside city itself, they walked unselfconsciously up the boardwalk ramp.

The first thing they felt, about half-way up, was the wind. At the top, the ocean breeze seemed to lessen the power of the sun. The air was crisp with sea-salt and their stomachs purred with hunger. Finally, they reached what appeared to be the lowest level of Ceca Hebona. They marveled at the minds that had created this maze-like, yet well organized system of platforms and roads made entirely of wood. And such wood! Not planks, but great, massive slabs of wood which had been soaked in some type of sealant. There was a thick, yet pleasant smell of some heavy, exotic oil.

To the left rose many levels which held a variety of buildings. Some were quite large, rising three or four stories tall, but most were single-level "homes". To the right, in the direction they were now turning, they stared at a wide, single-story building. A dark, colorful sign had been positioned above the main door; it said, simply, *Ceca Lo'Shoon*. Again, they heard the laughter and were drawn closer to this building. Beyond the structure was an unending series of ramps leading downward. Lincoln and Kayleigh moved toward one of these ramps. Looking down, they discovered hundreds of boats (in a wild assortment of shapes and sizes) docked at piers that jutted proudly into the Eastern Sea. The people who stirred among these vessels were not random about their business. They moved in a profound and well-rehearsed dance while the sun tossed golden sequins up from the water that swelled around them.

They turned as a bell sounded from behind them. Smiling, they watched as a large mass of children poured out of *Ceca Lo'Shoon*. Talking, laughing and some singing, they knelt in small, circular groups in front of the building and began to print words and other decorations on the well-weathered boardwalk.

Lincoln moved toward a younger group and saw that their writing was more simplistic than a nearby older group, yet still beautiful. Kayleigh stepped toward this older group (the average age perhaps ten years old) and knelt down with them. A girl with dark, auburn hair handed Kayleigh a piece of red chalk without even looking up.

"Thanks," Kayleigh said. She couldn't help staring at the girl. It was as if she'd seen her somewhere before.

"You're welcome," the girl said pleasantly, totally engrossed in her own writing. Kayleigh watched her, but could not decipher the characters she was printing. Lincoln joined them and focused immediately on the writing. His first thought was of all the strange symbols on the buildings back in Kana Hove.

"What does it mean?" Lincoln asked.

"It's David's new game," an older boy said, printing odd, thin lines and curves with a blue, chalk pencil.

"David Grey? Is he here?" Lincoln asked.

"Of course," the red-haired girl replied, chuckling. "He's back inside helping Meredith with the half-season students."

"I'll be right back," Lincoln said, then jogged over to the building.

The large room he entered was filled with hundreds of desks, though most of them sat unoccupied. Toward the center of the room, however, a group of perhaps twenty children sat in a semi-circle. All their attention was given to a teacher standing before them, reading from a book she held open in one hand. Lincoln just reached the outer border of the group when she looked up, smiled, then lowered the book quickly and stared hard at him.

"My, God," she said in an awed voice.

"Hi," Lincoln said lamely, then: "Is David Grey here?"

"Class dismissed," she said, her eyes focused only on him. The children collected their things quietly, filing out of the room without a sound.

Lincoln wanted to move his feet, but couldn't. Magnets of some alien origin held his feet in place. The teacher, younger now than he first thought, called out, "David! Are you in the back?"

"I'll be out in a second! I've almost got this thing working!" a voice replied.

A voice that made Lincoln's stomach flip ever so slightly.

"You're Lincoln, aren't you?" the young woman said softly.

Lincoln nodded.

They both turned as a boy only slightly older than Lincoln entered the open room.

"Ugh!" he said, "I can't figure out what these things do!"

Lincoln, being a certified computer fanatic back in the "real" world of Autumn Harbor, recognized the objects immediately. "Those are RAM chips," he explained. "They're a computer's active memory."

"No way! You know this stuff! Come here, I'll show you what I have so far—"

"David," the young woman said. "This is Lincoln."

David smiled, "Cool! Nice to meet you, Lincoln. Let me show you—"

"David," the woman repeated his name. "This is *Lincoln*. Our brother."

"What?" Lincoln started, the magnets releasing their hold on his feet. "Brother?"

"Awesome!" David said. He walked over and gave David a rough clap on the shoulder. "Now Meredith has someone else to pick on."

Meredith did not look amused.

David, ignoring his sister completely, ushered Lincoln away into a back room. The only piece of furniture inside was a large, square table. Lincoln drew in a breath at what he saw. Scattered about was a menagerie of electronic bits and pieces. Some were immediately familiar, though most looked as if they had been scavenged from some alien wreckage.

"So," David began, moving toward what appeared to be a standard desktop computer. "Explain again about these RAM chips."

Lincoln sidled next to him, looked down onto the exposed motherboard and pointed to an array of slots. "Start by putting one in right here," Lincoln instructed. "If you still get errors when you boot, put another one next to it right here and reboot. Sometimes you have to put them in as pairs."

As David began working with the chips, Lincoln looked closer at some of the other items on the table. Words on some of them were written in languages other than English, though nothing Lincoln had ever before seen or imagined.

"It looks like some of this stuff is from another world," Lincoln said.

Smiling, David looked up for a moment and said, "It's all off-world. I've been collecting these pieces from Traders. Normally, I have to keep it all hidden, but now that Mayor Stitch is gone..." His smile widened and he got back to work.

Lincoln picked up a smooth, metal cylinder about the size and shape of a sausage. Twisting the ends in opposite directions, the halves rotated and unscrewed completely. The hollow interior held a small, rolled square of paper; upon closer inspection, though, he saw that it was not paper, but some sort of soft, ultra-thin metal. Lincoln inspected both sides, but found nothing written on either. Setting the pieces back down on the table, he noticed a blue glow coming from a sphere housed in a sleek, black case. The globe reminded him of the strange lights in the Oak Hotel. A thin cable ran from the back of the black case to the computer David was attempting to reassemble.

"Yes!" David sighed, "Lincoln, check this out!"

Lincoln walked back to David and watched a flat, black screen fill with a hazy purple light. In a moment, a logo appeared: two iconic apples connected by three wavy lines. Below this were the words: *WaveMac OS-IX.*

"Weird," Lincoln breathed.

When the desktop interface appeared on the screen, however, it was familiar enough and Lincoln gave David a quick rundown of how personal computers in his world worked. In a matter of minutes (realizing that it was not controlled by a mouse or by touch) Lincoln tried several voice commands. Each time, a soft, female voice from a speaker embedded somewhere in the case replied, "This station is pass-phrase protected."

"The pass-phrase is 12345," Lincoln tried.

"Fail," the computer replied.

"Let me try something," David said, looking in his pile on the table for some obscure item. Lincoln looked up and found

Kayleigh standing in the doorway. Behind her stood Meredith along with two other girls.

"Lincoln," Kayleigh said softly, "They need to talk to you."

Lincoln turned to David and said, "I'll be right back." He followed the silent group down a hallway he hadn't noticed earlier and entered a room with another one of the low, square tables. Meredith and the two girls sat together on the far end while Kayleigh and Lincoln kneeled down before them.

"You said you had something important to tell Lincoln," Kayleigh began, watching as three pairs of eyes stared at Lincoln in wonder.

"Lincoln," Meredith began, "I don't know... you just..."

The youngest girl smiled and said, "We've been waiting for you."

Finding her voice, Meredith continued, "When I was much younger, I had to leave our home. There were people who wanted to kill our family, so my parents took us all very, very far away. There's an island out in the Eastern Sea, not that far from here, where we settled. Everything was fine for a while, but somehow they found us. Mother and Father put us in a boat and pushed us out to sea one night. Everyone else slept, but I heard the screams. Hours later, when all I could see was water by moonlight, I still heard the screams in my mind."

The two younger girls, perhaps fourteen and sixteen respectively, leaned into each other and held hands. Meredith continued, her voice weak but steady, "I tried to stay awake all night, to keep watch, but it was impossible. When I woke up, we had washed up on the shoreline near Ceca Hebona. There were five of us, Lincoln, but only four left that small boat."

"What happened to the other?" Lincoln asked, his voice shallow and his heart hammering.

There were tears in Meredith's eyes. She said softly, "I didn't find out until later how or why, but you had been taken from us. You, Lincoln. Our brother. And now, miraculously, you've returned to us! And you've brought with you the Princess Kell Korai."

Lincoln turned to Kayleigh.

"But how do you know about—?" Lincoln began.

"Wait," his best friend said wryly, patting him on the hand. "It gets better."

5. The Prophecy

hey sat talking for what felt like hours. Taking turns, Kayleigh and Lincoln had managed to retell their story, starting with their search for the mysterious book in her Grandmother's empty house. Before the three young women could begin their own tale, a bell rang, signaling the end of lessons. Lincoln felt an odd stirring deep within him at the memory of Ms. Ruttier ringing her brass bell an hour before closing up the library. Meredith, Kathryn and Nicole left to make sure all the children were safely off, promising to return.

"Are you okay?" Kayleigh asked.

"Sure… I guess. I mean, I've found my real family, so that's amazing, but I feel like there's something they're not telling us. Plus, I haven't even spoken to David about this yet and he's my brother."

"Why don't you go find him," Kayleigh said, "I'll stay here and wait for your sisters. You can bring David back here. Meredith told me some of what's going on, but we should probably hear the whole thing together."

Lincoln rose and retraced his way back down the hall to David's workshop. The older boy was still there, tinkering around in the fading daylight. Almost absently, he looked up.

"Oh, Lincoln, good. Come here. I've figured something out."

Lincoln walked over and noticed that David had attached a long ribbon cable from the motherboard of the computer to an odd, pentagonal-shaped apparatus which sat humming nearby. Wires ran from beneath the shell of this device to other equally anomalous gadgets positioned on the table.

"Check this out," David said, then spoke in a more formal tone: "What causes this computer to operate?"

The odd, feminine voice replied, "Three hybrid BioSynth liquid hafnium cores with superluminal field gate portals. Three Quads of active photonic memory are layered with—"

"Cancel," David said and the computer was silent.

"How fast is the CPU?" Lincoln asked.

"Each core runs at a relative speed of 300 Gigahertz per pico-cell—"

"Cancel," Lincoln said, his eyes narrowing. "This is way beyond me, but it all still looks like a regular old computer."

"I don't know what a regular computer looks like to you," David began, "But most of what's inside this thing is a lie."

"What do you mean?"

"Look here," he said, handing over what appeared to be an audio card. The casing around a chip on the board had been cracked open, revealing a thick, black gel that showed slow clockwise rotation.

"I'm not familiar with computers from your world, Lincoln, but I think there's a lot more going on here than we're seeing. I think all the good parts are hidden inside the old parts."

"Who would want to hide such amazing things?"

"Good question."

At that moment, Meredith leaned into the doorway. "I know you're excited about your new toy, David, but we're about to have dinner in the leisure room."

"Wouldn't miss it," David smiled. Meredith returned the smile and disappeared.

"I guess I should have come back to get you a while ago," Lincoln said apologetically. "We've been talking about how we ended up here. Your sisters (*our* sisters) were about to tell Kayleigh and I about what happened after you came to Ceca Hebona."

"Meredith doesn't like to talk much about the past, but I've figured a few things out. Have they told you about the prophecy?"

"What prophecy?"

"Something about our family having to unite with another family from our world. Apparently, it would bring ages of peace to Atoth, our planet."

Lincoln stopped, staring at David, "Did you say *Atoth*?"

"I think that's what it's called. There was a book Meredith remembers seeing when we were still on the island. It talked about Atoth, which I guess is the planet we came from."

They found everyone seated in the room and eating. Kayleigh gave Lincoln a questioning look, but he just shook his head. She pointed to a plate beside her own with a sandwich on it. Lincoln sat down, looked up at Meredith and asked, "Did you tell Kayleigh yet that our family comes from Atoth?"

"What?" Kayleigh asked, visibly shocked.

Meredith threw David a withering look. "Yes... that is something I wished to bring up when we were all together."

"You come from the same planet as my Grandfather?" Kayleigh asked.

"Yes. David? What else did you tell Lincoln?"

David, his mouth filled with bread and cheese, mumbled, "I might have mentioned the prophecy."

Sighing heavily, Meredith put her face in her hands. Kathryn straightened up slightly, attempting a genuine smile, "Why don't we just tell them and get it out of the way?"

Frowning, Nicole said, "This isn't something you just get out of the way, Katie."

Lincoln felt his legs go numb, but didn't move.

Meredith took a long drink from her cup, sighed again, then said: "Our family and the royal family of Atoth were to become one. Our family tree has produced the most brilliant of all Atoth's scientists. The royal Kell Korai line hoped to strengthen themselves against another family who claimed rights as the original royal family on Atoth."

"Let me guess," Kayleigh interrupted, "Truman Stitch is part of this other family."

Frowning, Meredith said, "Not directly, though he has allied himself with them."

"Okay, this is all interesting, but what's the big deal about this prophecy?"

"The prophecy was spoken over a hundred years ago by three blind sisters," Meredith said, looking up at the ceiling. "Many bizarre things they said were copied into the Town Notes, but not read until fifty years ago. What's so odd about all of this is that the sisters lived here on this planet, de'Na, not our own."

"So what does the prophecy say?" Kayleigh asked.

It was David who spoke, looking directly at Kayleigh, "It says that the eldest male in our family is supposed to marry the youngest female in a royal family. If they don't travel back to Atoth and claim their place as King and Queen, a great war will ensue, destroying hundreds of worlds before it's over."

The silence that followed was nearly complete. Kayleigh felt all eyes upon her; she turned to Lincoln. The look of off-centered panic in his eyes was all it took to move her to speech.

"Are you saying that David and I are supposed to get married? Our age, then, apparently doesn't seem to make any difference. And somehow we're supposed to go back to Atoth and save millions of people?"

"Billions," David added, "Though it's probably more like hundreds of billions." He then hung his head low at the withering look of his sisters.

Later, Lincoln found Kayleigh sitting at the edge of the boardwalk, looking down upon the piers. The view was spectacular: a full orange-cast moon hung motionless in a cloudless, mid-evening sky. The busy sound of gulls that had marked the daylight hours was gone. Other than the soft, foamy gurgle of the wake below, the only sound came from distant bells marking shallow areas in the surf.

"This whole marriage thing cannot be serious," Lincoln said, falling in place beside her.

She turned and faced him with a look that made him wish he hadn't spoken.

"Lincoln," she began, her voice dry, "Ms. Ruttier said that my Grandfather believed we were meant to bring back the de'Malange. She also said we needed to find someone called David Grey. Besides learning that you have family here, which is great, this whole thing about bringing two families together to save billions of people has got to be our main purpose. What could be more important or noble?"

"You sound like you *want* to get married to my brother," Lincoln said, smiling, and again wished he had just let her speak.

"Would you like to be our Best Man?" she asked with a smirk. "You can give David the ring that he'll put on my finger." She held her hand out to him, stretching out her left ring finger.

The full force of the situation hit Lincoln. His eyes widened and he reached out, taking her hand in his. "Okay, fine, no more wedding jokes," he said quickly.

Kayleigh laughed brightly, temporarily dispelling the solemn evening. They sat there, hand in hand, looking out over the final boats that were docking and the few that were launching from the lower wharfs. There was little movement.

"Of course I don't want to go," Kayleigh whispered. "I don't want to get married to David. I want to stay with you, Lincoln. I want to figure out what happened to my Grandmother."

Lincoln wisely chose silence, gently squeezing her hand. She squeezed back. They remained like this until Meredith found them, led them back to the school (which was also their home) and showed them to their rooms.

"Kayleigh?" a voice called from the doorway.

Kayleigh, who wasn't sleeping anyway, immediately sat up and rose from the thick mat she'd been given. Expecting Lincoln, she instead found David standing out in the hallway.

"Lincoln's waiting for us at the south entrance," David said quickly.

"Why?"

"We're leaving."

Kayleigh had a hard time keeping up with him; they took a roundabout route to the southern border of Ceca Hebona. Standing beside the same boat they'd slept under just the other night, Lincoln looked relieved upon hearing David and Kayleigh's footsteps moving down the wooden ramp.

"Okay, what's going on?" Kayleigh asked.

Lincoln only looked at David.

David took a deep breath and began. "Look, I know this all sounds crazy. One thing my sisters left out of this scenario is the fact that we have no way of getting back to Atoth. Whatever ship our parents arrived in is gone. Also, I'm not so sure about this prophecy. Meredith left out the fact that the Town Notes (all thirty-five leather bound books) are missing."

"Do you think those books might still be here in Burnam Tau'roh?" Lincoln asked. "Hidden? Maybe on the island our parents landed on?"

David shook his head. "Probably not, but going back there might give us some clues. Who knows? There might be something buried—"

"I highly doubt we're going to find a buried treasure filled with enlightening information regarding a prophecy given by three blind girls hundreds of years ago on an uncharted island," Kayleigh said in one breath.

"Besides," added Lincoln, "Won't getting there be difficult? I doubt these small rescue boats here would do the job."

David rubbed his right index finger and thumb together in deep thought. "We might be able to find someone who could take us there."

"No need to look far," came a voice from behind them. They'd been so focused on each other, they hadn't noticed the man holding a small suitcase as he walked up the beach toward them.

"Sagan, what are you doing here?" David asked.

"You know each other!" Lincoln said.

"Why does this not surprise me…" Kayleigh added.

"Who do you think keeps this young man supplied with his technology?" Sagan grunted, winking at David. "Anyway, I had a feeling I might find you all together. I'm glad your sisters aren't around, though."

"Me, too," David said, rolling his eyes.

"Well, at least it makes this all a bit easier," Sagan said, kneeling down beside the overturned rescue boat and sliding the small case over to them.

"More computer parts?" Lincoln asked.

David shrugged, though he looked deeply puzzled.

Sagan cleared his throat, then spoke again, more slowly:

"I must tell you something first, David. So you don't get too upset with me for keeping this from you. You see, I knew your father. I tried to help him, as a matter of fact. Tried to help all of you. I was playing double-agent with Stitch then, pretending to tell him about everything I saw and heard, but I kept my own little secrets. The Grey family was, perhaps, my biggest, most important secret.

"By pure accident, I caught sight of your parents' ship as it landed on that tiny island. From the highest lighthouse window, I watched it go down in the twilight. When I got there (it didn't take more than an hour by boat) your parents took a big risk and trusted me. I did my best to hide their location and throw Mayor Stitch off their trail, but I was out of my depth, so to speak. I was able to warn them an hour or so before Stitch found them. They managed to get you all away on that tiny boat. I don't think Stitch was even interested in you children. He wanted your parents."

David was staring down at the sand. Lincoln watched his new-found brother and wished he knew what to say.

"I was entrusted with this case and whatever items are inside. I was told, by your Father, to deliver it to the family when your brother returned."

"But," Kayleigh began, "That would mean their father knew that Lincoln was not going to make it to Ceca Hebona. He knew Lincoln was going to travel to a different world?"

Sagan lifted an eyebrow. "He certainly did. Lincoln," the man's voice grew more serious, "I was the one who passed you on before your brother and sisters were discovered."

"Passed me on?" Lincoln asked.

"Your father's instructions. I made sure everyone in the boat was safe. Then, right on time, a sailor named Creek appeared in a small skimmer and took the smallest of you," here he looked Lincoln dead in the eyes, "and took you back out to sea."

Putting her hand on Lincoln's shoulder, Kayleigh said, "When Stitch transported me out of Kana Hove, I appeared inside that creepy movie theater in the woods. Creek ran up to me in a panic and asked where you were. He said something about *In Soul Sea Grey*. Then Stitch appeared and zapped *him* away."

David's eyes brightened, "He must have meant Insoullsi'Grey, our family's true last name. Meredith shortened it to just *Grey* in Ceca Hebona... for obvious reasons."

"Well," Lincoln said, "This ties things together a bit more, but doesn't really answer any questions."

"Which is why we should probably open that silver case," Kayleigh said.

"Oh, yeah... about that," Sagan said softly.

"What now?" David's voice was low.

Sagan look slightly embarrassed, but he spoke anyway, "Beg your pardon, David. Lincoln. May I draw your attention to the small hole near the handle?"

David took the case and examined it. "It's probably for the key," he said.

Sagan coughed lightly into a clenched fist.

"I have a feeling I know what's coming next," Kayleigh said under her breath.

Sagan looked down at his feet and mumbled, "Yeah. Well... I lost the key."

6. Lock and Key

ayleigh, who had until then been the calmest of them all, felt her voice rise an octave. "You knew how important this was and you lost the key?" Lincoln could almost hear her heart (as well as his own) begin to race. So close, he thought. We seem to be so close…

"Hold on," David said, and soon they all saw that he was smiling. Still holding the enigmatic container, he continued to stare at it. "Sagan… what did the key look like?"

"Well," Sagan began, looking around the beach for inspiration, "I, uh… I'm not exactly sure. It was years ago, you understand."

David walked up to him and put a steadying hand on the older man's shoulder, "What I mean is—do you actually remember our father giving you a key?"

Sagan's brow creased, "Well… no, I can't recall him doing so, but he must have! I mean, why give me a locked case without the key?"

"Calm yourself, old friend," David said softly. Kayleigh stared hard at David, wondering what it was that made her so completely trust him. Because I know I shouldn't, she told herself. I shouldn't trust him at all!

Sagan finally looked up and met David's eyes.

"There was no key," David said, smiling, then turned to Lincoln and Kayleigh, "I think I know how to open this thing, but unfortunately it means going back and facing Meredith. She is not going to be happy about this."

"Sagan *did* say that this was supposed to be delivered to your family, right?" Kayleigh asked.

Lincoln glanced at David, knowing what they had to do.

Sighing, David handed the case over to Lincoln and announced, "I believe I should be the one to lead our sorry troop back up these wooden steps. Sagan, I thank you for staying true to your promise and helping to keep our family hidden and safe."

They turned to the older man, but the keeper of the lighthouse had already disappeared down the beach. He was no more than a charcoal slash against the grain of darkened sand.

By the time they reached *Ceca Lo'Shoon*, dawn announced itself as a bright cerulean line separating the sea from the sky. They all had a feeling Meredith would be waiting for them, though none imagined she would be standing there at the entrance of the building, Nicole and Kathryn at her left and right.

"I know what you're thinking," David began, mustering his most persuasive smile.

"If that's the thing our father left with Mr. Rideau, you should probably bring it inside," she said flatly.

"Okay... so I didn't know what you were thinking," David added, smile gone.

Walking down a now familiar hallway, Lincoln felt Kayleigh's shoulder bump into his. "Do you know what's going on?" she asked. Lincoln shook his head to the negative, "But I think I know how David's going to get that thing open."

"How?" Kayleigh said, eyes wide.

"Where are you going?" Meredith's voice was louder and less patient than it had been just hours before.

Reluctantly, they all followed David into his "workshop".

Testing the waters, though Lincoln thought his brother should have kept things on a more appeasing level, David asked Meredith, "Do you know how to open this case?"

Meredith only stared at him. Kayleigh was glad she wasn't on the receiving end of said look.

"Well," David began, "I'm certain that the hole here isn't for a key. At least, not a *physical* key."

"Stop showing off and just tell us," Kathryn said, yawning.

"No," Nicole finished. "Show us."

"Okay. Inside this hole is a tiny microphone. The key is probably a verbal pass phrase. Lincoln and I saw the same arrangement on a computer we setup yesterday."

"So give it the pass phrase and let's see what's inside," Meredith said, a bemused smile on her face.

"Oh, I don't know the password," he replied. The shock on everyone's faces could be felt more than seen. "Lincoln? I think you know where I'm going with this, right?"

Lincoln walked over to the hybrid computer they'd brought to life earlier and powered it up. He took the case from David and set it beside the many odd lenses and openings on the computer's now fully exposed front panel. David walked over to Lincoln and asked aloud:

"Computer? What is the pass phrase that opens this case?"

At first, there was only silence. Lincoln feared that something had gone wrong with the computer, but ten seconds later, the screen filled with a rapid flash series of schematics and what appeared to be mathematical equations.

"The pass phrase was never set," the female voice said. "Would you like to set one now?"

"Can't we just open it then?" Kayleigh asked.

"Negative," the computer replied.

"Okay, then," David said, "Please set the pass-phrase to..."

"Insoullsi'Grey," Lincoln finished. This brought a definite smile to both his newly found brother and sisters.

"Confirm pass-phrase to: Insoullsi'Grey?" the computer asked.

"Confirm," David said.

The screen blurred in a prismatic succession of multidimensional shapes, then went black.

"Pass-phrase has been set," the female voice said with finality.

David took the silver case and carried it almost reverently to his sisters. Meredith received it. Tears were visible in her eyes.

"How did you know about this?" David asked.

"Mother told me about it the night before we left the island. She said that one day, when we were all together again, father would send us important information. I knew that Sagan Rideau was our guardian."

She walked to a clear area in the room and knelt down on the floor. Everyone joined her. Leaning down, she spoke her family's true name and from within the mysterious case they heard a faint *click*. Taking hold of the lid, Meredith pulled it upward.

The first object caused both Lincoln and Kayleigh to groan aloud.

"What's the matter?" David asked.

Meredith reached inside and withdrew yet another copy of The History of Burnam Tau'roh. "How many of those things are there?" Kayleigh asked.

The second object was a tall, sealed glass cylinder. Inside were (at anyone's best guess) around fifty or sixty acorns. Meredith ran tentative fingers along the spotless glass hull.

It was Lincoln who spoke what they all were thinking. "Do you think those are from the de'Melange?"

"They wouldn't be sealed in such an impressive-looking container if they weren't," David offered.

"But why?" Nicole breathed.

Meredith removed the third and final item from the case. A sealed envelope.

"Does anyone want to—" she began, but Kathryn said, "Oh, just open it!"

The letter within was written in a beautiful, flowing script. For some reason, Kayleigh thought back to her meeting with her Grandfather, Emil. She was reminded of old secrets and uncovered truths.

"My Dearest Children," Meredith began. "There is simply too much to tell and my time is short. I have done my best to protect you and hope that one day you will read this. In my short time on this new planet, I have seen great contamination due to cross-dimensional trade. Such trade is punishable by death on our home world. Truman Stitch, perhaps the greatest of all contaminators, has run amok on this world. I admit that I must bend to Stitch's own practice if I am to keep you all safe.

Lincoln, the seeds contained within this heliodex will function as a powerful talisman and are entrusted to you. They must accompany you on your journey home. David, you must return to Atoth along with she who will help you mend centuries of suffering and future years of pain. The book I leave with you is a great enigma, but a powerful tool that should aid in your travels. I am certain that you have gained the necessary skills to unlock many doors. I know this is asking much of you, but it is all in the name of our family and our race. I wish I could be there with you now, but your mother and I must do our part to ensure your success. I'm certain you have all made us proud in whatever you are doing at present. We love and cherish you all."

A brief silence held the group captive.

Lincoln watched Kayleigh throughout the entire reading of the letter, seeing her expression grow more anxious with each word. He tried to take her hand, but she gently pushed him away. As soon as Meredith finished reading, Kayleigh stood. Her voice wavered as she looked at both David and Meredith. Finally, she said, "I'll go with you, David, but not before I speak with Mona Tarok."

"Kayleigh—" Meredith began.

"This is hard enough, but I need to—"

"Kayleigh, hold on," the eldest of them said soothingly. "I was going to say that I agree with you. We need an impartial mind to help us think through all of this. Mona Tarok is both wise and trusted. There must be some reason why we haven't been given concrete reasons regarding the prophecy. Otherwise, we would know exactly what to do."

At this point, everyone stood and moved toward the leisure room. David and Meredith left to gather a hasty breakfast while Nicole and Kathryn left to prepare packs for the two-day hike west toward the Oak Hotel. There was an odd chiming sound from down the hallway, then silence.

Alone in the room, Lincoln paced back and forth while Kayleigh sat staring at a fixed point on the table before her.

"This is completely insane," Lincoln said after a moment.

"I know," Kayleigh whispered.

"I'm going with you."

"No, you're not. You've got to stay here and help figure things out. My Grandmother—"

"But none of this makes any sense without you. We're in this thing together, Kayleigh. I—"

"Breakfast," Meredith announced, bringing in a large wooden tray with rolls and various berry spreads. She gave Lincoln an inscrutable glance before sitting next to Kayleigh and helping her with a roll. David and his sisters entered a moment later carrying three large backpacks, which they set against a wall. No more than ten minutes later, the bell rang and all listened as many eager voices began to fill rooms elsewhere in the building. Meredith, Nicole and Kathryn stood and offered hugs all around. They were gone without another word, tending to students who patiently awaited their teachers.

David was the first to shoulder one of the backpacks. He adjusted the straps, then stood at the doorway. Kayleigh and Lincoln retrieved their own packs and followed David out into the morning.

Their journey from Ceca Hebona to the Sughi River passed mostly in silence. They stopped briefly to eat in a wide field filled with the rusted remains of train tracks and scattered rubble, but otherwise walked without speaking. When they arrived at the river, however, David turned left, heading due west into the slowly deepening forest.

"Whoa, wait a minute," Kayleigh protested. "We're supposed to see Mona."

David stopped, heaved a sigh, then turned.

"Look," David said, looking back and forth between them. "You'll get to see Mona, I promise, but we have one important stop to make before that."

"Did this *stop* just occur to you?" Kayleigh asked, hands on her hips. Lincoln smiled. He enjoyed this passionate side of his friend, especially when it wasn't directed at him.

David took a deep breath. "I knew what we had to do as soon as I saw the heliodex."

"Kafír…" Lincoln said, eyes wide.

"If these acorns are truly the last seeds of the de'Melange, then I think we should at least speak with their only living relative."

"I agree," Kayleigh said, grudgingly, "But you should have told us."

David just stood there, staring at them.

"So," Lincoln said, annoyed with himself for feeling left out, "The plan, as I now see it, goes like this… We talk to Kafír Rosette. We visit Mona Tarok and see what she has to say. Then, basically, the two of you use the activation panel in that stupid book and travel to a planet on the brink of some insane civil war to save uncounted billions of people."

David stared at Lincoln with an enigmatic look that included traces of sorrow, apprehension and frustration. To make matters worse, Kayleigh turned to Lincoln and held up her hands as if to say *Was that really necessary?*

In the end, he only seemed to make their strained situation more awkward.

Again, they continued on their way in silence. Every now and then, David removed something from his pocket, glanced at it, then moved on—sometimes with a slight course change. Eventually, about an hour after they crossed the train tracks, they had to stop. The combination of failing daylight and thickening trees made it impossible to continue onward.

After a simple camp had been made, they sat facing each other in a loose huddle. Eating thick slices of sharp, tasty cheese, Lincoln found the courage to invade the silence, asking David, "Did you know about Kafir before we told our side of the story?"

David shook his head slowly. "No, but there's a story I heard when I was much younger. It's about a tree in the woods who dreamed of music. A child's bedtime story. The tree was called *Grande Okami*."

"So, until now Kafir Rosette was just a fairy tale?" Kayleigh asked.

David nodded.

"You're using a compass to guide us, right?" Lincoln blurted out.

David nodded again.

"Then please explain how you know which direction we should go. It would be like me trying to guide us through the woods to the cottage of The Seven Dwarves."

Kayleigh looked up at David with renewed curiosity, but Lincoln's new-found brother turned away at her glance.

Lincoln pressed, "You do know where Kafír is then. How?"

"No more arguing," Kayleigh said softly, putting an arm around Lincoln's shoulder and pulling him close to her. David stood and moved off a few paces into the trees. Kayleigh leaned in close to Lincoln so that their foreheads touched. The unexpected closeness caused Lincoln's heart to race. Kayleigh's words were but whispers, but they filled his world. "Don't ask how I know, but things are not going down the way we planned back at the school. David's whole attitude changed after we opened that briefcase. I think he's holding something back."

"We should get some sleep," David said, causing Kayleigh and Lincoln to jump. They had not heard him return.

Kayleigh stretched, then pushed back onto her bedroll. "Goodnight," she said.

Lying on his own sleeping bag, Lincoln tried to see the stars between slowly shifting tree boughs high overhead. He recalled the last time he and Kayleigh had fallen asleep in these same woods. He leaned over toward where Kayleigh slept and whispered, "I thought the deal was that I got to use your shoulder next time..."

But there was no response from his dear friend.

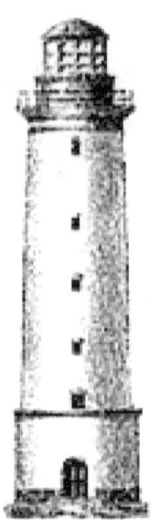

7. Grande Okami

t was odd waking to near darkness, but the clouds above were heavy and the air smelled of rain. After a hurried breakfast, they were off again, following David as he conferred with his compass. Sometime before noon, they came into a clearing and David stopped.

"This isn't good," he said.

"What's wrong?" Kayleigh asked.

"She's supposed to be here."

They all looked around, but the clearing was empty.

"I don't remember Kafír being in a clearing like this," Lincoln said.

"That's right," Kayleigh added, "She was more like… in the middle of everything."

David checked the compass, then spoke impatiently, "I'm not talking about the tree."

Lincoln and Kayleigh exchanged a look of bewilderment, then jumped as a voice spoke from the other side of the clearing.

"He's talking about *me*," said Sheenie, emerging from a dense cluster of bushes.

For a while, no one said anything. Sheenie walked over to David and stood before him. Neither spoke, though information seemed to pass between them. After a pause, the mysterious woman moved past him and walked toward Lincoln.

Smiling, she said, "I did not anticipate seeing you again so soon, but I am glad of it. Greetings to you, Kayleigh."

Kayleigh nodded.

"It's good to see you too, but what are you doing here? And how do you and David know each other?"

"David and I haven't met until just now. We communicated for the first time a day ago."

Lincoln's eyes widened, "The computer! That sound we heard the last time we were in the school… that was you trying to communicate with David?"

"In a way," Sheenie said, "It was my ship. Truman had modified both our ships to search constantly for any new signals that might emerge over the eastern sea or in the planet's atmosphere. He didn't want a single clue to pass him by. When you two activated that computer, my ship picked up its broadcast and alerted me. Through the computer, David told me briefly what was happening and I told him the part I've been playing all these long years."

"So what do *you* think we should do?" Kayleigh asked. She wanted to believe that this woman was on their side, but she couldn't totally trust her.

"Well…" Sheenie began.

"I think we should wait until we speak with the tree," David interrupted.

All three turned to him as he backed slowly toward the northern edge of the meadow.

"That's probably a good idea," Sheenie said, taking Kayleigh's hand and leading her toward David. Lincoln followed as their party (now four) reentered the thick woods.

Kayleigh's heart sank at the thought of having to travel further through the forest, but it was only a half hour later when they stopped. Moving past Lincoln, Sheenie and David, Kayleigh walked up to the grand sight of the last of the de'Melange. She reached out to set her open palm against the trunk, but stopped.

Something was wrong.

She turned to Lincoln.

"I feel it, too," he said.

They looked up into the wide boughs above them.

"Kafír?" Kayleigh called, "Kafír Rosette, we have returned!"

They waited. David and Sheenie moved closer, then stopped behind them.

Finally, a breeze blew down from the cool morning sky.

"Ah, my children," said the tree, each syllable created by the complex movement and interaction of leaves and branches caressing each other in the wind. "I was hoping we would have this final meeting."

"What's wrong?" Kayleigh asked.

"When you invoked the Pandiment of Travel and the portal opened between worlds, the abomination poured its thoughts through the breach and I was infected."

The air grew still.

"The abomination was Ka Tolerates," Kayleigh said quickly to David.

Sheenie sighed, "It still is Ka Tolerates. It has infected Truman as well, augmenting every selfish and evil intent."

A stronger wind began to push through the woods.

Kafír continued, "When the evil returned to this land, I tried to close my mind to it. Still, it found me. Even after it has left us, I fear I have little time remaining."

Kayleigh knelt down, shrugged off her pack and withdrew the odd jar of acorns.

"Kafír, are these acorns of the de'Melange?" she called out.

Impossible as it should be, the great tree appeared to straighten as if to stand at proud attention.

"Kayleigh and Lincoln, you must return this heliodex to Emil Kell-Korai. It has lost its way. Much rests on this request I so humbly ask of you."

"But my Grandfather is dead, Kafír. He was killed by Truman Stitch."

"He was murdered by Ka Tolerates through Truman Stitch," the tree said softly, "Nonetheless, you must return these seeds to our keeper. You must also deliver our lost and forgotten souls in the vessel of darkness. The de'Melange must sing again."

"What—?" Lincoln began to ask.

Kayleigh quieted his words by reaching out and taking his arm, pulling him toward her. She looked in his eyes intently, trying to communicate an important detail, though it was completely lost on him.

They waited for another breeze.

A few random raindrops began to translate from low clouds.

"I will rest for now, children. We shall speak once more before my time is up. My gift to you will be one final Pandiment."

With these words, the wind died down completely and a heavy, unforgiving rain began to fall.

Using their bedrolls, David and Lincoln fashioned a crude shelter under a nearby stand of tall bushes. They worked quickly, but all were well soaked by the time it was done.

"Okay," Lincoln said, rain dripping from his hair and nose, "What was that about a *vessel of darkness*?"

Kayleigh leaned forward, "You still have that tiny bottle Mona gave us, right?"

Lincoln frantically began patting his jeans, then stood hunched under the shelter and shoved both hands in his pockets.

David and Sheenie looked on curiously.

Breathing a sigh of relief, Lincoln sat down and handed Kayleigh the bottle.

"That's a bottle?" David laughed.

Smiling, Kayleigh said, "It's dark and it's a vessel."

"A very small vessel," Sheenie, who had very little to say, added.

"Kafír didn't say anything about size," Lincoln whispered.

Lost in her own thoughts, Kayleigh said, "It must be made of something more than simple glass, otherwise we'd be able to use any old bottle."

"Mona might know more about it," Lincoln offered.

Sheenie shifted on the ground, "You should probably see Shipmaster Creek. He is free now and has access to much information now that Truman is gone."

"Is he still at the Cinema?" Kayleigh asked.

Sheenie smiled, "Yes, but it is more than just a Cinema."

"It has mini golf now?" Lincoln asked.

Frowning at Lincoln, Kayleigh asked, "Did you know that Shipmaster Creek took Lincoln to Autumn Harbor when he was a baby?"

Sheenie looked hard at Kayleigh, "Creek is a good man. I regret much of what I have done to him for my brother. I am ready to do what I can to change things."

Suddenly, Lincoln understood.

"You're from one of those royal families," he said, looking at the young woman, "You're like Kayleigh, the youngest daughter in your line. You're going to leave with David."

Sheenie looked from Lincoln to Kayleigh. "Our families intersect four generations ago. I am the only daughter in my branch of the family. I can fulfill the prophecy as well as Kayleigh. Besides, Kayleigh has more important things to worry about."

"How can you say something like that?" Kayleigh asked angrily, "How can you know? Anyway, what could be more important than saving billions of lives?"

The rain slowed with a preternatural suddenness, then stopped completely as a blast of wind blew through the trees and nearly tore apart the hasty shelter.

A familiar voice broke through:

"Children! To me!"

"Kafír!" Lincoln said as they all took off toward the tree at a run.

Kayleigh reached the ancient tree first. "Kafír, what is it?"

"I fear... I fear the sickness is... taking over."

The wind pushed against them with greater strength; an inland gale. Lincoln moved closer to Kayleigh and asked, "Do you think the same thing that happened to Ka Tolerates will happen to Kafir?"

Kayleigh did not want to think about it.

"How can we help you?" Kayleigh screamed through the wind.

"Do as I have asked. Deliver the heliodex. Return our lost and wandering souls."

Kayleigh felt like crying. She'd never felt so helpless. So lost...

"We will!" she called out. "I don't know how, but we will!"

Sheenie stepped up, her voice strong, "Kafir, can you accept one last Pandiment?"

"No," Kayleigh said, a look of outrage in her eyes, "She's dying!"

"You must speak quickly," Kafir's voice strained. "I haven't... much time..."

"I thought we were going back to Atoth on your ship?" David asked, taking hold of Sheenie's hand.

The young woman smiled sadly, "Even if we were able to sequence the trip at hibernation speed, it would take nearly three years."

David's brow creased as he considered this, then asked, "But Truman—?"

"Truman is no longer human. He can push his ship to speeds fatal to you or me and still survive. This is the only way we can hope to arrive before him."

Sheenie turned to Kayleigh and Lincoln. "You must see Creek. Anything he doesn't know he'll be able to find out. Your questions will be answered with him."

Somehow, Kayleigh thought, I doubt that.

"Now…" Kafír moaned weakly.

Sheenie and David, still holding hands, stepped up to the great oak tree. Sheenie spoke aloud:

"O Deliver Me,

"Twilight deep within the wood,

"Across the great void"

As she recited these words, long, black cracks began to slide up and down the gnarled trunk. Kafír seemed to be holding something inside of her, keeping some terrible thing in check. Lincoln's body shook as he recognized the sound coming from her. It was a simple thing, and so heart-breakingly human. She was sobbing.

"We wish to go to the Applewhite Estate in Alhambra Minor on the northern continent of Atoth."

A spinning oval of soupy, spectral light grew from a point on the tree before them. It slowed when it was no bigger than a beach ball and they all feared that the Pandiment would fail, but Kafír pulled in some final reserve of energy to extend the portal. When the opening was about four feet high and two feet wide, Sheenie and David pushed through it together. The rotating liquid of the gateway slowed, then stopped. The portal seemed to glaze over. What life remained in the tree was nearly gone. The raging wind was no more than a light breath now.

Lincoln and Kayleigh stepped back, gasping as they watched the enormous tree slowly pull into itself. It didn't shrink so much as compress in complex and dizzying geometries. Some hidden entity was sapping all life from their friend, eating at her goodness and devouring her pure spirit. Tens of thousands of leaves fell from above like slow, joyless confetti. Within minutes, Kafír Rosette was a crackling shell of carbonized wood.

Kayleigh fell to her knees less than a foot from the tree and reached out with her open palms.

"No," some final, conscious part of the tree hissed. There was no longer a mechanism to control the sound of words.

Communication was accomplished through some other means, perhaps directly into their minds. "Do not touch me, Chaska. Things would get quite nasty for you if you did."

"Kafír?" Kayleigh asked.

"She is gone, gone, gone, but one final wish remains. She told me... no, she commanded me... yes. I am to tear myself apart, fleeting ones. I am to unmake myself. We who inhabit the xylem and phloem... Father says to leave it alone, but it's so... pretty. Mother is sleeping forever. We must touch Wicapiwakan! Hide and seek!"

And then the tree that was once Kafír Rosette and the last of the singing oaks, a true de'Melange and the fabled Grande Okami, began to unravel before them. The bark tore away in ribbons that spun and burned to grey embers on the forest floor. The sound it made was soft and horrible. A book destroying itself page by page immediately after the author has written THE END.

Lincoln's skin prickled at the sight and he jumped when Kayleigh grabbed his arm and pushed her face into his shirt. He felt her crying as he continued to watch the tree shred.

In one great downward motion, the main trunk collapsed upon itself, causing Kayleigh and Lincoln to stumble and fall backward. The ripping and tearing continued for perhaps a minute longer, but soon all motion stopped. The deadfall of timbers gave one, final sigh and Kafír Rosette was no more.

Standing again, Kayleigh and Lincoln listened to the wood, but there was silence. Kayleigh walked toward a lone branch that appeared to be reaching out from beneath a larger section of curled and splintered wood. Each smaller twig radiating from the end of the branch were like yearning fingers. Kayleigh held out her hand.

"No," Lincoln breathed, but Kayleigh touched the branch anyway, running her fingers along the dry wood.

"I was able to use Ka Tolerates one last time to leave Te'hæra Thorn," Lincoln said. "Do you think—?"

"No," Kayleigh whispered, "There's nothing left."

Joining Lincoln, drying her eyes on her sleeves, she said, "Let's find Shipmaster Creek. I'm tired of not getting the whole story. We need to know what's going on and what we're supposed to do now."

As they pulled together the scattered remains of their camp, Lincoln noticed and picked up a tiny acorn from beneath a patch of moss. It was still green and fresh, fully intact. He showed it to Kayleigh.

"Do you think this was from Kafír?" he asked, placing it in her hand.

Kayleigh offered a small smile, but said nothing and placed it in her pocket.

Lincoln glanced around. "I know it was dark, but wasn't that the way we came from the Cinema the last time we were here?" He pointed across the small clearing to an opening in the woods.

Kayleigh nodded.

A warm breeze came from the south, pushing gently against them, urging them onward, but this time there were no whispered words to accompany it.

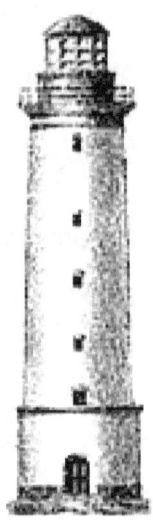

8. Descent

Although they had the compass that David left behind, they never took it out for reference. The further they traveled through the forest, the more pronounced the path became. Eventually, when it was nearly noon, the trail grew quite narrow, then opened up onto the back lot of the Cinema. The rear of the building was completely in shadow. The only sound they heard was the disquieting chirp of a lone cricket.

Moving cautiously around to the front, they looked down the familiar overgrown road to a multitude of small, ominous cottages.

"Man, even during the day this place is creepy," Lincoln said.

Kayleigh turned back to the façade of the Cinema and the row of movie posters. "Let's just get inside," she said.

Everything within was exactly as Lincoln remembered it. There was even the soft, muted snap of popping corn and the aroma of butter. The man they sought was sitting on a red velvet couch on the left hand side of the lobby.

"I had a feeling I'd be seeing you two sooner or later," said Shipmaster Creek. He wore dark blues and greens. A long, grey cloak darkened his frame further.

When neither Kayleigh nor Lincoln spoke, he stood and moved toward the main counter.

"It wasn't you we met the last time we were here," Lincoln said.

"No, son, that wasn't me. Stitch had me tucked away."

The old man walked around the concession counter and pulled open the glass door of the popcorn caddy. He pulled a wax-lined tub from under the counter and filled it with popcorn.

"Kafír is dead," Kayleigh said flatly.

Creek set the tub on the glass counter and sighed.

"I know. Don't ask me how 'cause I couldn't begin to tell you. Some part of me just knew when it happened earlier today. Are Sheenie and David gone? Did Kafír let them through?"

Kayleigh was silent, so Lincoln answered, "They're gone. Kafír said she was infected by Ka Tolerates through the portal she opened for us."

"I figured it had something to do with that. When you two first came here, Truman locked me up. When he left, Sheenie let me out. She told me what happened and where you'd gone."

Kayleigh walked over to one of the red loungers and sat. "Sheenie said that you'd have some answers for us."

Taking Kayleigh's lead, Lincoln sat down beside her and asked, "You knew my father?"

Creek sighed again, put a few pieces of popcorn into his mouth and chewed thoughtfully. Leaning on the counter, he began:

"Your father and I were best friends, Lincoln. The night we met, I was mending sails on the northeastern docks in Ceca

Hebona. It was a cloudy night and there was deep thunder out over the Eastern Sea. It was the thunder that masked the sound of his ship as it fell from the sky. I looked out over the waves and watched this curved thing hover over the water, then race eastward. Packing up my sails, I launched my swiftest boat and took off after it, knowing how crazy I was.

"I found you and your family on one of the many unnamed islands out there. Another man, Sagan Rideau, joined our odd party. Those first few weeks, I ferried food and other supplies from the mainland to Khan. That was your Dad's name, Lincoln. Khan Fetrig Insoullsi'Grey."

"What was my mother's name?" Lincoln interrupted.

"Roquet Meneh," Creek said softly. "They loved you all so very much. While I helped your father build your home, basically a reinforced entrance to a cave in the center of the island, he told me about the Applewhite Regime on their planet, Atoth, and how they were trying to gain total power by silencing all religious and scientific voices."

"By silence, you mean kill, right?" Kayleigh said.

"Yes," Creek agreed. "And by any means possible. Very few families or groups were able to leave the planet. Those that did were hunted down. Truman and Sheenie were just two of many hundreds of bounty hunters trying to gain favor with the Applewhites. What's so despicable about Truman Stitch is that he was from one of the greatest mathematical families. He betrayed them all to save himself. Sheenie Tosh (not technically his sister, but a distant cousin) was the only one left on her side of her family. She only recently regretted the mistake of siding with him."

"Unless," Kayleigh put in, "She stayed behind as a spy and has fooled us all, taking David back into more danger than any of us can imagine."

Lincoln sat straight up and stared at her.

"Come on," she said, "Don't tell me you never thought that. Truman gets all freaky and evil, so why *not* let him take off. She brings David home and is the instant hero."

"How come you never mentioned this to David?" Lincoln asked, anger painting his words.

"I did. During the storm, I pulled him aside."

"What did he say?"

"He shrugged. He said that it was his duty to go back. He said he would be able to fix things. He said it's what his… *your* parents would have wanted him to do."

Lincoln leaned back into the cushions, "He obviously didn't need any help from me."

"I hope you don't mind me saying so, Lincoln," Creek chimed in. "But you and Kayleigh have some pretty important things to do here."

"Yes," Kayleigh agreed, looking back at the sailor, "All of which you're going to tell us about right now, starting with my grandmother."

Shipmaster Creek pulled a small, red chaise over to the couch, along with two more tubs of popcorn and tall waxed-paper cups of Cherry Ace soda. The three of them sat facing one other, munching and sipping and the rest of the world could have passed them by.

"Most importantly, I will tell you this, Kayleigh. You're grandmother is alive and well. I'm afraid I can tell you nothing else. With good fortune, if things work out the way they should, you will see her before too long. Please, don't look at me like that. I know that sounds unfair, but it's the truth. Now, Lincoln, getting back to your side of the story for a moment... Like I said, many Pilgrims left Atoth. We can only guess that most were hunted down and killed. Keeping your brother and sisters a secret, especially so close to Stitch, has not been easy, but hiding in plain sight has seemed to work. Convincing Truman that all of you children sank with that small boat was stretching the limits of persuasion. I don't think he ever fully believed it, but with the help of Sagan, we did our best.

"Now, I have to ask… do you have the heliodex? Good… wonderful! Hiding that thing was the next most difficult thing in this whole affair."

"We also have another copy of The History of Burnam Tau'roh," Lincoln added.

"Oh, no," Creek groaned, "Don't tell me your parents put one in that case. Those books can all go to flame! It is a recording of truths as well as lies. Those books are the only things in this whole mess we can't figure out."

"Well…" Kayleigh redirected, "What can you figure out?"

Calming himself, Creek said, "As long as the heliodex is safe, it doesn't really matter, I suppose."

"So they really are acorns from the de'Melange?" Kayleigh asked.

"Yes. From what we've pieced together, they are a very important item in completing this whole quest."

Digging in his pocket, Lincoln pulled out the small, dark vial. "We think that this is another important item."

Creek nearly choked. "Where did you get that?"

Kayleigh cleared her throat, "Apparently, a sick man left it for us at The Oak Hotel. He must have known we were going to stop by one day."

Lincoln dipped into his pocket again and pulled out the coin, passing it to Creek. "He also left us this."

"Interesting," he said, "Once, this was coin of the realm, though it hasn't been used around here for a long time." He handed it back to Lincoln. "But this vial…"

"Kafir said something about containing souls in it," Kayleigh said.

"Yes. Yes, exactly. So much has been written about this. No… I will get to that later. For now, I'm just thankful everything is starting to come together. Put that tiny, precious thing safely away."

"So what is our ultimate goal in all of this?" Lincoln asked, "This whole craziness started with Kayleigh's grandmother going missing, but what…? Bringing the de'Melange back? Is that it?"

"Is that *it*?" Creek gasped. "Do you realize how important and near impossible doing such a thing is?"

"So that *is* the big thing we need to do," Kayleigh said, more to herself.

"Why couldn't someone else do it? Why the two of us?" Lincoln added.

Shipmaster Creek rose, setting the now empty tub on his seat, "Come. I will show you how I know what I know."

Kayleigh rose next, leaving her snacks behind, but Lincoln hesitated. "Can I bring my drink?"

Creek and Kayleigh stopped and turned. "If you promise not to spill it on anything," the old man said, hiding a smile.

They were led down one of the two main hallways, both of which opened into the theater.

"Whoa," Lincoln said softly upon entering the large room. The theater was immaculate. The seats were leather with brass accents. The floor was carpeted in waves of rich reds, browns and oranges that channeled the deepest autumn. The curtain that hung before the screen was a dark burgundy and simply begged to be stroked.

"You like it?" Creek asked.

"It's absolutely amazing," Lincoln said.

"But this isn't what you want to show us," Kayleigh put in.

"No," the old man said soberly. "Just a bit further."

They followed him to the far side of the auditorium, toward the fire door, which was labeled with a glowing, red *EXIT* sign. Through the door, they found themselves in another, smaller hallway that moved at a gentle slope downward. After twenty feet, the hall made a sharp right turn and went on for another twenty feet. At the end, they faced an odd door fashioned from some dark wood. Burned into the center of the door were many detailed engravings—leaves and flowers. Lincoln held back the urge to reach out and touch the tiny marks.

Creek spoke softly, "Level one, please. Authorization 8677287MD5."

The door, which only a moment ago appeared so solid, split vertically down the middle and slid effortlessly open. Creek stepped into the elevator and they followed. The door closed and the cab moved silently downward, stopping only a few seconds after it had begun. The door *shushed* open.

"Merry Christmas," Lincoln said through a wide smile.

They walked into the most spectacularly decorated room, though it felt more like a dance hall than a mere room. Hundreds of fir trees, each decorated differently, filled the vast area before them. Soft music filtered down through hidden speakers: an instrumental rendition of The Twelve Days of Christmas. Scattered between the trees were small piles of wrapped presents, tables set with candies and cookies. Kayleigh and Lincoln walked slowly, as if this were the surface of some alien world rather than an ornately blandished hall.

Lincoln, who had stopped at a table piled high with frosted cookies turned back to their host with a grin.

"Sorry," Creek said, "They're not real. Everything here is just for show."

"But why?" Kayleigh asked.

"Well…back when I took Lincoln through one of those floating bubbles to the world you both grew up in, I stayed on for a few months, just to make sure he was being taken care of. Khan asked me to do this. At the end of my time in Autumn Harbor, it was December and your Christmas holiday was coming up. I'd never heard of such a thing!" He turned to Lincoln, "I stayed an extra week, keeping my eye on you and your new family, just to see what this *Christmas* was all about. It hit me so hard, the feeling of happiness that seemed to fill every corner of the town. People were happy. Things just felt charged with excitement. I left your world on Christmas morning, Lincoln, just after I watched you and your parents through the front window of your home. You were all sitting on the living room floor and they were helping you open your presents. You weren't even two years old. I knew then that everything would be okay for you."

Lincoln's body felt as light as a warm breeze listening to the older man's words. He felt as if his heart had traveled back through time.

"But…" Kayleigh said softly, aware of Lincoln's feelings of nostalgia. "This isn't what you want to show us, either, is it?"

Creek shook his head. "No. But I'm glad I was able to show you. This whole building was constructed with Truman's money and influence. He wanted a place to store all information regarding Emil and the Pilgrims. He didn't want to miss a single clue that might lead him back to them. There are many underground levels beneath the theater. This is only the first."

"How many are there?" Lincoln asked.

"Seven. At least, seven that I know of. I've always wondered if Stitch had something hidden a bit deeper. Anyway, level seven is where we need to be."

They walked back to the elevator and Creek asked for the seventh level using the same authorization code. The elevator traveled downward for the slow count of ten, then stopped. Kayleigh and Lincoln smiled. They couldn't help it. The door opened to a room they both knew very well.

9. The Note

They stepped from the elevator out into the main lobby of the Autumn Harbor Library.

"How is this possible?" Kayleigh whispered.

Lincoln, on the other hand, was calling out for Ms. Ruttier.

"Hold on there," Creek said, smiling, "We're not in Autumn Harbor. We're still beneath the Cinema."

Lincoln turned to him.

"It's a reproduction," Creek added.

"This isn't our library?" Kayleigh asked, confused.

"Well, it is and it isn't. Come over here and I'll show you."

He led the children to a study cubicle. Sitting on the desk was a very thin laptop computer. It wasn't plugged in, but the screen was on. Lincoln recognized the desktop graphic. It was the same as the computer he and David had managed to boot up back in his brother's makeshift workshop.

Creek sat down before it and Lincoln and Kayleigh pulled chairs up next to him at either side.

"Stitch used this to store and cross-index information. It's the most advanced computer that's come through any of the bubbles. It can access any other computer in this hemisphere of the planet and automatically download information into its own memory. Most of what it gets comes from Traders passing through."

"Do you know about David's computer?" Lincoln asked.

"Your brother was not supposed to get his hands on something so powerful. Fortunately, Sheenie found out and made contact. I would have liked to give them updated information about Atoth before they went back, though. Who knows what they're walking into."

"Does this computer work by voice, too?" Lincoln asked.

"Yes," Creek replied. "Stitch named the thing Taira Han, after his mother. So... Here we go." He leaned slightly forward. "Good evening, Taira Han. It's Creek."

Kayleigh looked across at Lincoln and smiled at the politeness with which the man spoke. The voice that answered was similar to that of the computer David put together, though more refined, as if this computer was older and wiser.

"VoicePrint confirmed. Good evening, Shipmaster Creek. How may I help you?" it asked.

"I'd like to introduce you to my new friends," Creek said. He turned to Lincoln and said, "Just tell her hello and say your name."

Clearing his throat, Lincoln spoke first, "Hi, Taira Han. My name is Lincoln Torres."

"Welcome Lincoln Torres."

"Hello, Taira," Kayleigh said next, "I'm Kayleigh Lambert."

"Welcome Kayleigh Lambert."

"Taira," Creek said, "could you please pull up all the information we've collected on the Pandiments."

"Of course. One moment, please."

The screen dimmed. Behind the cubby, floating in the air, a flat rectangle of light appeared. Lincoln guessed its dimensions to be about six feet long by four feet high. The computer seemed to pass its display over to this new, larger area. On the floating screen appeared many virtual folders broken down into different categories. All concerned Pandiments: *Basic Pandiments. Earliest Pandiments. Forgotten Pandiments.* Kayleigh and Lincoln scanned the screen in wonder, wishing they could read it all at once.

"Okay," Creek said, "Please list files in *Forgotten Pandiments* by date of discovery."

The screen cleared and a short list of Pandiments filled the screen:

1. Pandiment of Conditional Convergence.
2. Pandiment of Spherical Harmonics
3. Pandiment of Integral Transposition Functions
4. Pandiment of Chronodimensional Confluence

"Well?" Creek asked. "What do you think?"

They stared at the list in wonder and confusion.

"I'm not sure what we're supposed to be seeing," Kayleigh said, eyebrows narrowed.

"Is there going to be a test on this later on?" Lincoln asked. "I feel like I'm back in Mr. Tegeyo's math class."

"Number four," Creek pointed, "Chronodimensional Confluence. Time manipulation."

"You mean, time *travel?*" Lincoln asked.

Lincoln and Kayleigh rose and followed Creek across the lobby toward the children's literature section. Lincoln couldn't get over how similar, down to the smallest detail, this place was to his favorite library.

Creek knelt before a low shelf of picture books. He chose a small, square book: *The Story of the Painted Lighthouse*. They all sat down on the multicolored rug and leaned slightly in toward each other.

"Forgive me if I'm telling this out of order or in the wrong order... there's so much to say and I don't want to mess it up..."

Smiling like a child who had just won a race against a group of older rivals, he opened the book and flipped carefully through the pages until a scrap of paper appeared between pages 12 and 13. He pulled it out and offered it to Lincoln.

Taking the paper, Lincoln stared at a familiar logo... one that appeared on the crates in the basement of the Oak Hotel. Kayleigh recognized it, too.

"Trokamano Orchards," Lincoln said. "This looks like one of the papers they used to wrap the fruit before they put them in the crates."

"Turn it over," Creek whispered.

Lincoln did. Kayleigh leaned in close and they both read the familiar handwriting:

Kayleigh & Lincoln,

Okay, we are now returning our own favor. There is much for you both to discover on your own, but we were told this was one of the Key Elements. The Pandiment of Time is kept by the Three Sisters. They will trade for some candy. You must make this trade and leave a letter exactly like this one in a safe place. The Pandiment is: Many directions... In a dark and frozen sea... Are forever yours. Do not return to Kafir. Do not return to the Oak Hotel.

Kayleigh & Lincoln

"That's your handwriting," Lincoln said, looking up at Kayleigh.

"But knowing this Pandiment does us no good. Where are we supposed to recite it?" Kayleigh asked, already diving into the logic of the situation. "If this letter has come from the past, then I'm guessing we'll have to go backward in time."

"When Truman first had me gathering information (when I started my career as a double-agent that is) it included collecting nearly every available book in Burnam Tau'roh. When I cataloged each book, I did a quick inspection. I found this note in an old tome about orchard tree pruning and rapture figs. I think I bought it off an old farmer on the western side of the woods."

"So this letter has been sitting around for quite a while, then," Kayleigh said.

"But how long exactly?" Lincoln asked. "There are no more de'Melange left and the note says not to return to Kafír, or whatever is left of Kafír. Even if we found another tree like her, we don't know what time to travel to or where these Three Sisters are."

"Well..." Creek said, "I can help with part of that. Truman was a very shrewd man, but this note was the one thing I kept to myself. I handed over everything else I found, which really wasn't much. One of those things, which I discovered before I found your note here, was a letter written over one-hundred and eighty years ago from a worried mother to Mona Tarok. Her three daughters, on the morning of their third birthday, woke up blind. Their mother was searching for help. She was desperate."

"What happened?" Kayleigh asked.

"I don't know. There was only that one letter. But it mentioned three sisters, like in your note."

Kayleigh was pacing with the note in her hand, staring at the words as if some hidden sign were eluding her.

After a moment, Creek sighed. "I'm not really supposed to tell you this, but you left a note for me, too."

"What did it say?" Lincoln said.

"You told me not to say."

"But you just did!" Lincoln said, infuriated.

"I know… but there's this thing that happens to you. Both of you. Something horrible. I'm not sure how it turns out. I just wanted to tell you… be careful, okay?"

"Is there anything else you can tell us? Did this other note mention anything about my Grandmother?" Kayleigh asked.

Creek looked uneasy, was about to say something, then shook his head no.

"Is Mona Tarok from one of those scientific families? Was she born on Atoth?" Kayleigh asked the old man.

Creek looked surprised by the question. "No. I don't believe so."

"So then either you're lying or something's really wrong. You said the letter about the Three Sisters is from over a hundred years ago. Mona Tarok can't possibly have been alive back then if she's here now in our time, unless she has a longer lifespan than we do."

Creek said nothing.

"Fine. Lincoln, let's go."

"Where?"

"Back to the Oak Hotel. We need to speak with Mona."

"But didn't we tell ourselves not to do that," Lincoln said worriedly.

"Is there anything else you can tell us?" Kayleigh asked Creek.

"Just don't do anything until tomorrow morning. Shora Cessyu is awake."

"The last time we were here, you said there were spirits or something out there," Lincoln offered.

"That wasn't me you spoke with," Creek explained, rubbing his tired eyes. "It was Stitch, but spirits are as close an explanation as anything. I don't really know the nature of the folks in that little town. They're really protective of those houses, though. I've been tempted to go inside one (you know... during the day?) but I never had the nerve. Stitch never talked about them and I never asked."

Kayleigh's manner changed instantly.

"So we can sleep here tonight?" she asked.

Smiling, Creek rose and pointed to the other side of the room where many long, comfortable looking couches lined a red-brick wall. "You're welcome to any of them. I can even bring down some pillows and blankets."

"That would be great," Kayleigh said. "Thank-you."

Creek, happy to be of further help, turned toward the elevator with a bit more life in his step.

"Hey, wait!" Lincoln said, running to catch up. "I'll help."

Kayleigh moved slowly back toward the desk and Taira Han. Just before the elevator doors closed, she heard Lincoln ask, "Could I have another cup of that Cherry Ace stuff?"

Later that evening, at what time neither could guess, Lincoln sat at an empty table with *The Story of the Painted Lighthouse* open before him. Kayleigh sat on one of the couches, a thick, blue blanket wrapped around her.

"How many times are you going to read that?" she asked.

"I don't know," Lincoln replied, "I just have a weird feeling that Creek put that note in this book for a reason."

"He did," Kayleigh said.

"What do you mean?"

"Is there a picture in there that shows a door at the top of the lighthouse stairs?"

"Um... no. Not that I can see."

"What does it say about the light at the top of the lighthouse?"

Lincoln turned to another page and read, "The fresnel lens at the top of the Painted Lighthouse is controlled by autonomous means and only needs a human caretaker to make sure that the *ForeverBatteries* in the basement are dry and safe."

Kayleigh was smiling. "There *is* no room behind that door," she said.

"Sure there is," Lincoln countered.

"How do you know?"

"Well... aren't there normally rooms behind doors? Or closet spaces? Or... something?"

Kayleigh only smiled.

"Okay, then how do you know it's a fake door?" Lincoln asked.

"I asked the computer."

"But Creek shut it down when he left. And isn't it protected by a VoicePrint or PassPhrase?"

"I asked the computer while you two went upstairs to get our bags, the pillows and food."

"But won't Creek find out? Won't Taira tell him?"

"She might, but that's not important right now. I think you're right about Creek choosing the Lighthouse book for a reason. I even think he left me alone down here on purpose."

"So? What's up with the fake door, then?" Lincoln rose and moved toward Kayleigh's couch.

"It's not a fake door. It's just not a normal door. I'm not totally sure about this, but from what I just learned, I think that the door at the top of the lighthouse is, in part, made of wood from a de'Melange tree."

Lincoln nodded. "We still don't know what happened to all those trees in the valley," he added. "Or what was done with them afterward."

"Taira doesn't know much about what happened on Te'hæra Thorn, either. I think she learned a good bit from what I had to tell her."

"We might be able to confirm some of this when we talk with Mona tomorrow."

"We're not going to see Mona."

Lincoln sat down beside Kayleigh and stared at her.

"I take back what I said," Kayleigh explained. "I think we were correct in our letter about not knowing too many things."

"So you *weren't* supposed to learn about that door by talking with Creek's computer?"

"I don't know. It's not like we snooped around and found the second letter we left for him."

Lincoln's eyes brightened.

"No," Kayleigh said, learning toward him. "It's a tempting idea, but it could be hidden anywhere down here. Or somewhere else completely. There are many floors we haven't even seen. We should just get some sleep. I have a feeling tomorrow is going to be very interesting."

"Since when have our tomorrows *not* been interesting?"

Kayleigh leaned closer to him.

"We're going to have to be careful," she said.

"I didn't like what Creek said about something really bad happening to us."

"We can't think about that or we'll go crazy."

"Still…"

"I know."

"What do you think our parents are doing?"

Kayleigh shook her head. "We really can't think about them right now, either."

"Do you think they would understand what we're doing?"

"I think they know that, whatever happens to us, we'd always try and do what was right."

They broke apart, staring at each other with a million questions.

Smiling, Lincoln retrieved his own blanket and sat back down beside her, leaning gently against Kayleigh's left side.

"I would have died if you left with my brother," Lincoln whispered.

Kayleigh said nothing at first. Lincoln thought she'd fallen asleep, but then he heard her whisper:

"I know now that I would never have let that happen."

10. The Pandiment of Time

They left Shipmaster Creek just as the sun broke through what remained of yesterday's storm clouds. After helping them restock their backpacks with food and other random supplies he thought they might need, he returned from the concession counter and tossed in a few boxes of PopTop Taffy. "For your trade with the *sisters*," he said. They told him about their idea concerning the door at the top of the Painted Lighthouse. The aged sailor said nothing, but nodded and seemed to sigh with relief.

Though they had David's compass, both were unsure of the exact direction they needed to go to reach the Painted Lighthouse. They decided on a north-east path toward the Sughi toh' Lodare river. The river, they knew from experience, would take them directly to the sea and the lighthouse.

It wasn't long before they came to the northern section of the Burnam Tau'roh Eastern Rail line. If anything, it seemed even more unused and overgrown than before.

"I guess we won't be meeting up with BTEL #3 today," Lincoln said, looking up and down the tracks.

"Probably not," Kayleigh said.

They reached the Sughi before noon. Sitting on the shore of the river, they ate an early lunch.

"Cool! Look!" Lincoln announced, taking a large square of folded brown paper from his pack. Inside was a large portion of popcorn.

"It's all yours," Kayleigh said, smiling. "I'm done with popcorn for a while."

Upriver, to their left, they could see the rise of a small mountain. It was difficult to make out, but the Oak Hotel sat at the top, the smallest mark against the sky.

"Are you sure we shouldn't take another day, or two, and see Mona?" Lincoln asked.

Kayleigh answered at once. "I'd love to see Mona. It would be nice to ask her a few questions without being hunted down by Stitch or having to leave in a hurry. But we have to get to the lighthouse. To that door."

"It's going to work," Lincoln said seriously. "You can feel it, can't you?"

Kayleigh shuddered. "I can feel something coming."

With lunch done, they continued eastward, following the shore of the river. Their progress was mostly downhill and each time they reached a rise in the land, they could look downward and see the sparkle of the Eastern Sea. Instead of talking about what might await them, they spoke about "normal" things. They talked (and worried) about their parents. About the new movies that were supposed to be out during the holidays. They wondered what their friends were doing at that moment.

"They're probably at home doing homework," Kayleigh said.

"That sounds so much more exciting than time-traveling into the past," Lincoln said.

"Especially if it's social studies homework," Kayleigh added.

"True," Lincoln laughed, knowing that social studies was Kayleigh's least-liked subject. "Do you think we'll ever get a chance to work on that project you told your parents about?"

"If we don't, we'll have a heck of an excuse."

And on they traveled.

They did, as they had hoped, reach the lighthouse before sunset. This time, however, there were no costumed dancers romping about and no music. The only sound, keeping time with their hearts and breath, was that of the sea. The surf. The soft, sibilant rush of waves.

The sun, now on its downward arc toward the western horizon, threw thick, orange light against the white exterior of the lighthouse, making it stand out even stronger against the storm-dark sky over the sea. There was only the faintest, distant rumble of thunder.

"What do we tell Sagan?" Kayleigh asked.

"The truth," was Lincoln's reply. "He risked his life for my family. The least we can do is to tell him the truth."

Though Kayleigh had been finding it more and more difficult to trust anyone lately, she had to agree. Unfortunately, Sagan Rideau was nowhere to be found. They searched the outer perimeter of the lighthouse and the beach. They found a small room beneath the main level (accessible from outside behind the main entrance) where Sagan might have lived, but the room was empty. There were no personal items that would have led anyone to believe someone was living there.

Back inside the lighthouse proper, they moved directly to the staircase that spiraled toward the top. From where they stood, they could not see the door high above. The light from the setting sun, pouring through a handful of evenly spaced windows, brought the many paintings on the interior wall to life. Entranced by the artistry before them, they began their climb toward the top.

The first mural depicted a land of deep forests filled with odd-looking creatures. Many of them had the faces of apes, though their skin was a translucent blue and two broad, lacy wings sprouted from each of their backs. The trees they flew around, easily ten times the width of Kafír, had many large holes dug into their trunks. Upon closer inspection, Lincoln saw that a few of the flying apes were emerging from these holes.

"The trees are their homes," Kayleigh whispered. Lincoln nodded.

Ten more steps and the mural began to change. The trees of the forest shifted to blue and morphed into a sun-spangled sea. Upon this sea were large boats with great multihued sails. They appeared to be moving in groups across the water. As they had seen on Te'hæra Thorn, there were two suns in the sky, though both were smaller than Earth's sun.

"Those aren't boats," Kayleigh said.

Lincoln moved closer to the wall and realized that Kayleigh was correct. The boats were marine creatures. He noticed two eyes on either side of their heads and multiple blow-holes on their backs. The sails were actually great flaps of skin that rose from their sides, attached to long, bony appendages. The flaps caught the wind and possibly helped to warm the creatures by absorbing the faint light from the binary stars.

The higher they climbed, the more bizarre and amazing and beautiful and impossible the paintings became. There were creatures that resembled humans in every way except one. Instead of hands and fingers, there were soft, mossy sponge-like masses. The people in this area were harvesting some type of grain in a field, their blurry hands carrying large bundles of stalks from a field and lining them up in concentric circles.

Halfway up the stairway they saw massive painted insects float in the vacuum of space, connected by thin filaments. The hazy strings, they imagined, were the roads upon which the insects traveled, connecting the many worlds hovering at varying distances.

Up, up and up.

The scene of a beach at night, though nothing so friendly and inviting as the beach just outside the lighthouse. The water appeared not only black, for the sky was ink-black, but thick and soupy. Also, there was no surf. The water sat still in a dead line against the shore. Lining the left hand side of the mural, with long pegs piercing the sand, was an uneven, tilted boardwalk. Again, in contrast to the breathtaking boardwalk structure of Ceca Hebona, this was more of a poor afterthought. Both Kayleigh and Lincoln slowed toward the middle of this section as a sick feeling of dread filled their hearts.

"No, don't stop," Kayleigh said, more to herself than to Lincoln. "Keep moving. I really don't like this one."

It took all their willpower to push onward and not be swallowed by the diseased power of the dead beach and the rotting boardwalk.

When they finally escaped it, their footsteps grew quicker.

Bright purple birds with two pairs of wings flew in circles around an active volcano.

Men and woman, human as far as they could tell, walked on the floor of a lapis sea without the aid of breathing equipment.

Dozens of creatures with the face of a tiger and the body of… well, something like a platypus, crawled over a small hill, tending to nests of black and orange striped eggs.

Upward still they climbed until the setting sun's lambent light turned to dark blue and then purple. As they walked the final twenty steps, the murals were nothing more than grey smears that might have been accidents, yet held great secrets.

And then there were simply no more steps, only a platform with barely enough room for both of them. The tall, wooden door before them was no more than a black outline against darkness.

They reached out and set open palms against the wood, hoping that touching it would make the door seem more real. The rough grain and random knots helped to ground them.

"I just did something bad," Lincoln said.

"What?"

"I looked down."

"Why in the world did you do that?"

"I was wondering if I could see the floor from up here."

"Could you?"

"No. It feels like we're floating. I'm afraid to take a step anywhere."

"Let's just say the Pandiment before anything else can happen."

There was a silent moment, then Lincoln groaned. "Man," he said, "How are we supposed to read the Pandiment without any light?"

"Calm down. I memorized it."

"Really?"

"Are you ready?"

Lincoln didn't answer. Instead, he reached out, found her hand and squeezed firmly.

"I'll take that as a yes. Okay, here we go."

She took a full breath, hoping to calm down, not wanting her voice to shake.

And then she recited:

"Many directions
"In a dark and frozen sea
"Are forever yours"

They waited in darkness.

They waited, hands tightening.

"I think I see some—" Lincoln began, then jumped as the black world around them erupted in a bright, painful strobe of light. When their vision returned, the door was now visible only as a razor-thin, white rectangular outline. Within this outline, they slowly recognized a familiar chaotic rotation of pearly darkness. It was the same eerie swirl from the activated portal in Kafír.

"What point in time should we ask for?" Kayleigh whispered.

Lincoln's eyes grew wide. "We didn't tell ourselves in that letter, did we?"

"Maybe an exact time isn't that important. We know we need to meet these Sisters, right?"

A moment of thoughtful silence.

"Um… I was thinking…" Lincoln's voice was thin.

"I know what you're going to say," Kayleigh turned to him, pulling him close. "It hurts for you to go through. But what if we go through together? Holding hands. Both hands, even?"

"I don't want you to hurt, though."

"I'm willing to take that risk. Are you ready?"

Lincoln swallowed hard, then nodded.

Kayleigh turned her head to the portal and said, "Take us to a time in the past where three blind sisters lived in Burnam Tau'roh."

The portal shook. The rotation quickened.

"Let's go," Kayleigh said.

Still facing each other, both hands tightly clasped, they sidestepped toward the door. Pushing at the cool threshold, there was a moment of hesitation, of being stuck.

Then they dropped and there was only the horrible, disorienting feeling of free-fall.

They opened their mouths to scream, but there was no sound.

Only falling.

Their stomachs wobbled during this brief moment of vertigo and just as quickly as it had begun, the downward journey was over. They hit the water hard, sinking below the surface. Letting go of each other's hands, Kayleigh and Lincoln kicked upward toward the light above them. This wasn't easy with their packs strapped tightly to their backs. Coughing, spitting dense, salty water, they broke the surface and felt the powerful movement of the surf push them toward the shore. Treading water, the packs now acted as flotation devices and carried them onward.

Crawling up onto the shore, wiping sand from stinging eyes, the two travelers scanned their surroundings. The first thing they noticed was how narrow the beach was. The beach they had just left seemed to stretch a good half mile from shore to dune. The waves that struck this new, younger shore here were of a fiercer nature. The dunes, taller and less worn, began only fifty or so feet from the surf in tall banks of closely packed sea oats.

"Um… where's the lighthouse?" Lincoln asked.

"It's got to be here somewhere," Kayleigh said, scanning the beach.

But the lighthouse was gone.

"We fell straight down from where the lighthouse is supposed to be," Kayleigh said, looking back out over the water. "Whatever time we're in, the tides and the land are in different positions. I don't think the lighthouse has even been built yet."

"But what time are we in?"

Kayleigh shrugged, heart racing. They climbed the high dune and left the beach behind. In a matter of minutes, the sun would rise over the horizon of water and sky.

What if we've gone back too far? Kayleigh thought. I should have been more specific when I spoke to the portal.

They noticed a small figure rising over the western edge of the dune. There was a voice, too, though they couldn't hear it until the child was almost upon them.

The girl was about their age and wore a simple homespun dress and sandals. Her hair was pulled back and tied in a loose knot. Tears pooled in her eyes. She moved past Lincoln and nearly threw herself at Kayleigh.

"You must come," she said, her voice cracked and dry.

"Where?" Kayleigh asked.

The girl tried to speak, but couldn't regain her breath. "Please," she managed to say, then turned and ran west.

Without thinking, Kayleigh and Lincoln followed the girl until the dune leveled out onto more solid, less sandy ground. What they saw caused them to stop and stare. Instead of an open field (which would eventually turn into the Eastern Woods) stood a building raised upon tall, mortared stones. The roof was highly pitched and its many narrow windows were propped open with sticks. They began to walk slowly toward it.

"What *is* it?" Kayleigh wondered aloud.

"It's a train station!" Lincoln said excitedly. As soon as he said this, Kayleigh noticed the tracks. They emerged from the west and turned sharply around the building, disappearing toward the northwest. As they moved closer, she also saw the sign on the side of the building facing south:

The Burnam Tau'roh Eastern Line
Ticket Station III

They didn't notice the girl until they were almost upon her at the entrance of the building. Her face was dusty and tear-streaked. Her head was tilted at an angle registering impatience. The long, deep blast of a horn filled the distance, muted slightly by the onset of the woods.

"The train will arrive in a moment," she said.

"Who are you? What's going on?" Lincoln asked.

"My name is Rylyn. It's Mona—" the girl said, trying to hold back another sob.

Just then, a magnificent train emerged from the distant woods and began to slow, brakes squealing as it neared Ticket Station III. Sunlight glinted off each polished angle of the hulking vehicle.

Rylyn tried to speak, but her tears began anew.

"What about Mona?" Kayleigh asked. "Please tell us!"

"She's dying," the girl finally said and fell into Kayleigh's arms.

To be continued in…

Queen Of
The Oaks

The Chronicles of
Burnam Tau'roh
Book Three

Pronunciation Guide

Burnam Tau'roh – bur-NAHM TAH-row

de'Na – day-NAH

Kafir Rosette – ka-FEAR roh-SET

Te'hæra Thorn – tuh-HAY-rah THORN

Ka Tolerates – KAH toe-leh-RAH-tays

Kana Hove – kah-nah HOVE

de'Malange – day muh-LAHNJ

Mona Tarok – moe-nah TAIR-ok

Kell-Korai – kell kor-EYE

Shora Cessyu – shor-ah say-SOO

Ceca Hebona – see-kuh heh-BOW-nuh

Grande Okami – grand o-KAH-me

Cast of Characters

Kayleigh Lambert – A twelve year-old girl from Autumn Harbor. Kayleigh is on a quest to discover the secrets of her Grandmother's past.

Lincoln Torres – A twelve year-old boy from Autumn Harbor. He and Kayleigh are best friends.

Laura Corwin – Kayleigh's Grandmother.

Lea Ruttier – The Autumn Harbor town librarian.

Mona Tarok – The cook and keeper of the Oak Hotel.

Truman Stitch – The corrupt Mayor of Burnam Tau'roh. He has been infected with the soul of Ka Tolerates.

Sheenie Tosh – Truman's sister (cousin).

Sagan Rideau – The keeper of The Painted Lighthouse.

Shipmaster Creek – The proprietor of The Cinema in the forgotten town of Shora Cessyu.

BTEL #3 – A locomotive train that runs on the Burnam Tau'roh Eastern Line.

Kafir Rosette – A mysterious, sentient tree hidden deep in the woods of Burnam Tau'roh.

Emil Corwin – Kayleigh's Grandfather.

Ka Tolerates – An evil tree that inhabited the Valley of the Oaks on Te'hæra Thorn.

David Grey – Lincoln's brother.

Meredith, Nicole and Kathryn Grey – Lincoln's sisters.

Walter Klimczak is the author of *Falling in the Garden* and *This Place Only*, the first two books in the TimeFront series. He lives in Atlanta, Georgia with his wife and three children.

www.ingramcontent.com/pod-product-compliance
Lightning Source LLC
Chambersburg PA
CBHW020731210626
46807CB00016B/1337